Miss Rose's House

The Spirit of Miss Rose

Book One

By

C.S. Martin

Acknowledgements

I would like to express my appreciation to the caring people who assisted me in bringing Miss Rose's House to fruition and publication.

Thank you so much to the members of the Circle of Christian Authors (CCA) writing group, who valiantly read early chapter drafts and offered useful suggestions. Thanks to my editor and long-time friend Jaye Denaman, for her expertise in polishing the manuscript while maintaining my author's voice and story. The charming cover was designed by graphics artist EDH Graphics, and I thank her for the diligence with which she depicted the setting that arose within my imagination. Many thanks, as well, to Sara Benedict for formatting the manuscript. Most of all, I would like to thank Kristi Osbourne for her encouragement and help in the publishing world. Each of you helped bring my story to life on the screen and page, and I appreciate your individual endeavors.

On a personal note, deepest gratitude and love to my family for their unwavering belief in me and constant support. They are my greatest fans.

Carolyn S. Martin

Miss Rose's House
by
CS Martin

Chapter One

"When I get through with you, no other man will ever want you!"

Will's threat reverberated through Emily's mind, even though the man himself was far behind her in Kansas as she drove toward the Oklahoma-Texas border and sanctuary. The vision of his red-suffused face contorted by rage as he screamed those vicious words seemed ingrained on her brain. Heaven knew they'd intruded on her conscious thoughts over and over throughout the long drive.

Whether or not he would have followed through on his warning she couldn't guess and hoped she would never know. After that final menacing shout, he'd whirled around and rushed through the apartment door, slamming it behind him so hard a framed photo fell off the mantle and hit the hardwood floor, its glass shattering.

Ironically, the picture was one of Will and Emily soon after she arrived in Kansas. As she brushed the glass shards and all other traces of the photo and frame into a dustpan and headed for the trash bin, she reflected that perhaps the smashed picture was an omen. The relationship was certainly damaged beyond repair.

That quarrel was the last straw for Emily Parker. She'd never been the victim of physical violence by Will Forrester—only the verbal abuse he dished out whenever he didn't get his way—and she had no wish to add bruises or broken bones to the painful memories of her time in Kansas.

She phoned her daughter, rented a small haul-it-yourself

trailer from an all-night truck stop, packed and loaded before daylight. Will had not returned—he was no doubt holed up with his friends getting plastered while complaining about how misunderstood he was. With any luck, he'd pass out wherever he was and give her time to make an escape before he surfaced again.

Her luck held. There was no sign of Will when she sent her boss an email with an apology for quitting her job without notice, but pleading an out-of-state emergency (and, in Emily's book, being physically threatened by a man who had sworn that he loved you was a genuine emergency). She had a feeling Genna, who'd met Will a few times and was unimpressed, would read between the lines. Still, Emily was sorry to leave her in the lurch with no advance warning.

It was nearly eight o'clock when she drove away from the small apartment complex, dropping her key into the mail slot at the office with a note … heading away from Kansas and the disappointment of Will. Heading back toward Texas. God's country.

Where I'll stay, she vowed.

She stopped at a convenience store to gas up and get some sandwiches and bottled water for her small cooler, so she would only need to stop briefly during the long drive for bathroom breaks and to stretch her legs. The time she spent sending necessary text messages to close out her residence in Kansas meant it was past nine-thirty when she finally left the city and entered a lane of the interstate highway.

The sinking autumn sun cast shadows onto the dashboard of Emily's SUV when she drove across the Oklahoma border into Texas. It had been a long, grueling trip, but her first sight of the red, white and blue "Welcome to Texas" sign with its familiar flag made all of her fatigue worth it.

—

At last! Back where I belong, she thought, *and I'll soon be with Miranda.*

The weight of anxiety that pressed on her during the wearying drive from Kansas through Oklahoma lifted at the thought of seeing her very pregnant daughter. Cedar Valley, the small town where Miranda and her husband lived, was now less than an hour's drive away.

Turning west onto Highway 55, Emily mused about the bumpy road she faced—not the highway, which was freshly resurfaced and smooth, but the dual undertakings of finding a job and a place to live in a town where the small size limited work opportunities and available real estate. She wanted to live close to Miranda, especially with the baby's birth imminent. Anything else was open to compromise now that she was back in Texas after purging her life of the worst mistake she'd ever made.

Home—it was a glorious word that produced a wonderful feeling. Had it been only a couple of days since she'd despaired of ever being happy again? How amazing that the welcome sign of her home state engendered such profound emotion and filled her with optimism. Welcome to Texas, indeed! Emily Parker was going home.

When she was younger, Emily considered small town life boring, but after the misery she'd fled, the prospect of living in a small town seemed inviting. Too much of the wrong kind of excitement had blighted her recent past. If a boring environment and even a commute were in her future, so be it. There would also be a loving daughter to reconnect with, a terrific son-in-law who adored Miranda, as well as Emily's first grandchild due in a few months.

"Don't worry about anything, Mom," Miranda had said when she phoned to pour out her heart. "You can stay with us as long as you like. I'm so relieved you decided to cut your losses and leave

---

Will. He pretended to be a nice guy so you would follow him to Kansas, but I always had my doubts, and now he's shown his true colors. When you've got more than four hundred miles between you and his temper, I can finally stop worrying."

It saddened Emily that her safety was a source of concern for her daughter. Miranda had enough on her plate with a baby on the way and a novel to finish writing prior to the birth. She didn't need stress spilling over from her mother's problems.

When she hung up from the call, Emily vowed not to let her stress interfere with Miranda's and Jared's life together. They were so happy, looking forward to their baby, with Jared's accounting business going well and Miranda reaching the goal of publishing her fiction. Emily would not mar their happiness by dwelling on her breakup with Will or the mess that preceded it.

What was that slogan her dad used to say every morning to get her excited about school? "If you want a positive attitude, just fake it until you make it." Emily had proven often enough in her life that the concept worked. Now it seemed she would get in a bit more practice faking confidence until the real thing showed up.

The first task on my to-do list—even before finding a job and a place of my own to live—is to regain my sense of wellbeing. Will's selfishness, his bad temper, taking advantage of me financially ... She shuddered, thinking of his excesses. *He nearly destroyed my self-esteem, and no man is worth that price. Thank God I came to my senses.*

Emily was relieved she'd stashed the proceeds from the sale of her Texas home into a savings account before moving to Kansas. Even though she'd trusted Will in the beginning, for some reason she never mentioned those funds to him. Perhaps her subconscious knew he wasn't reliable and protected her from her own generosity when she still thought him worthy of her love.

Now that money represented security to help her get settled again in Texas.

Emily hoped she would find a job as fulfilling as the marketing coordinator position she gave up in a Dallas suburb before moving to Kansas. It was likely she'd have been promoted to manager there by now if she'd stayed.

Maybe I'll put some feelers out with that company again. I'm eligible for rehire if they have the right opening. It's not too far to drive from Cedar Valley.

Independence was a word with a nice ring to it. The word would be her mantra as she rediscovered focus and contentment for her life. Emily's intention was to be independent and responsible for her own happiness—not to depend on some unreliable man to make her happy. She'd tried that since being widowed, and where had that gotten her? After having a happy marriage, it was difficult to let go of the belief that not all men could be trusted like Chris.

Honey, she thought, visualizing his dark hair and laugh lines, *I never told you enough while you were alive that you were a terrific guy. Well, I hope that where you are now, you can read my thoughts and know how much I loved and appreciated you. I'm beginning to think there's not another man on this earth who can hold a candle to you. My recent experience showed me that much. Perhaps I should stop looking and just be thankful for the years we had together.*

She recalled Miranda's admonition, "Love can mess with anyone's judgment, Mom. The important thing is that you take a step toward the future and let go of the past. Think about the new grandbaby you'll soon have to cuddle instead of what happened in Kansas."

Emily knew her daughter was right, but it was difficult to banish painful memories. For months she'd struggled to patch the failing relationship with Will. It was like trying to build a house with duct tape instead of nails. She knew now her attempts were destined to failure because he was fixated entirely on himself. One partner cannot save a doomed relationship if the other doesn't care.

The brutal showdown with Will began when she said no to his expectation that she'd subsidize another of his grandiose schemes for making it big in the music industry. It ended with him yelling accusations and threats before he stormed out and banged the door against the wall. Will was a narcissist. He would never love anyone else the way he loved himself, and Emily knew she deserved better in a partner. Crossing the border into Texas made their break official. It was over.

She eased the SUV and loaded trailer into Miranda's drive, turned off the ignition and rested her head on the steering wheel. Shivering, she buttoned her cardigan at the neckline, unsure whether the cold creeping into her bones came from the autumn temperature or the thought she was alone again.

Lights flickered on, visible through the kitchen window when the café curtains fluttered. Emily got out of the vehicle and reached for her overnight bag. Miranda walked down the back steps, pulling a heavy knit shawl around her shoulders, and headed toward the silver vehicle, her thick brown hair pulled into a ponytail held by a thick scrunch, her ear-to-ear grin visible even in the dim lighting.

She wrapped her arms around her mother's neck, and Emily returned the hug, conscious of the solid baby bump between them. She was rewarded by a kick. Despite the huge belly, Miranda felt too thin in her arms. Tomorrow she'd start cooking the favorite comfort foods Mandy loved as a child—dishes that would pique her appetite and nourish both her and the developing baby. Mac and cheese, chicken and dumplings,

—

stewed potatoes with peas.

She needs me here, Emily thought. *A woman wants her mother nearby when she's preparing to give birth for the first time, and I'm so glad I'll be here for her.*

She followed Miranda into the house, agreeing with her daughter that they should wait until morning to unload the remainder of her things.

"You must be exhausted from the long drive, Mom. I've got your bed ready, so get a good night's sleep. We can catch up on talk in the morning."

Flannel sheets on the antique bed felt soft and warm, the plump down mattress inviting. Emily quickly drifted into slumber, but her dreams grew chaotic during the night, reaching a peak of subconscious alarm in the early morning hours.

In her dream she ran frantically through a house while heavy footfalls sounded behind her: "Thump, thump!" She didn't know who was trying to catch her, couldn't see her pursuer's face, but this phantom seemed to get nearer as she desperately tried to escape. She ran and ran through the dream landscape, but made no progress. At times her feet seemed too heavy to lift, while at others they moved backward like a moonwalk.

I've got to get away!

Even as her subconscious mind screamed the thought, a different part of her brain recognized she was not in her waking world, but in the grip of a nightmare. Even so, she couldn't shake off the frenetic mood or evade the sinister illusion.

Chapter Two

"Mom!"

The sound of her daughter's voice broke through the dream fog to her conscious mind. Startled awake, she saw Mandy standing beside the bed peering at her. Sunshine filtered through the curtains.

"Breakfast is ready, Mom. I hated to wake you, but you had a frown on your face. Bad dream? Well, strong coffee with pancakes and bacon will chase away the dream monsters. I'll put your plate in the oven to warm while you dress."

When Emily walked into the dining room, breakfast was on the table and Miranda was pouring hot coffee. Her son-in-law, Jared, rose from his chair and hugged her before she sat down.

Miranda was in what Emily called her bossy mode.

"Get with it, you two. We need to get all the stuff unloaded and take the rental trailer to the drop-off place by noon."

"There's nothing heavy to unload," Emily said, "just my clothes, kitchenware and bathroom stuff. Don't you remember? I left my furniture in storage when I moved to Kansas and lived in a furnished apartment there. Perhaps my subconscious saw Will was a bad bet and protected my antiques for me. I can now imagine him selling them for whatever he could get."

"Well, you can stay here as long as you need. There's lots of room in this house, and we'll love having you here. I've missed you so much, Mom."

Miranda and Jared had been married three years and expected their first child in February. He'd inherited their home from his grandmother, and they lovingly renovated it before starting a family.

11

In addition to the pregnancy, her daughter was also birthing the first volume of a three-book historical romance series for which she'd signed a publishing contract. She wanted to finish the first book before the baby was born, and the holidays were approaching. Emily knew her daughter's schedule was full and didn't want to encroach on her time. The highly-organized Miranda, however, already had plans.

"I've spread the word among my friends that you're looking for a job and a house, plus I drove around yesterday and found a couple of houses nearby with "For Sale" signs. One is a block off the main street and only a few blocks from here. It would be a short walk to our house. It's a charming place with two bedrooms.

"Rose Loving—Miss Rose, everyone in town called her, even though she'd been married and widowed—lived there until she passed away about six years ago. She left the house to her son, Garrett.

"I don't know why he held onto the house so long before putting it on the market, because he isn't likely to ever live there himself. He lives in Dallas and also has a ranch here, just a few miles out of town."

Emily and Jared smiled at each other as Miranda chattered on about the Loving house. When Mandy got on a roll, she could out-talk anyone in north

Texas. Her mom and husband wouldn't even try to inject a word until she paused for breath.

"I'll give him credit," she was saying. "He doesn't stint on upkeep. The utilities are kept on—for six years now, mind you—with the thermostat set at a comfortable temperature. A lawn service keeps the grass cut and shrubs trimmed every summer. I know all this because Garrett hired a friend of mine to clean the house every week. Cassie says it's still furnished just as it was when Miss Rose died. She was told to clean it as thoroughly as if

---

someone still lived there. I think that's kind of weird, don't you? "

That afternoon, mother and daughter pulled into the driveway of a small cottage a few blocks from the town square. Emily liked the two mature oak trees that gave the impression of sentinels guarding the house, one on either side of the walk. The trees' massive trunks confirmed their age, and their outstretched leafless limbs met across the concrete walkway, leaving shadows on its surface.

White shutters graced the front and side windows on the driveway side, a pleasing contrast to the light tan brick facade. A wooden privacy fence hid the back yard. It wasn't a large house, but it looked big enough for her needs, and Emily noticed a chimney rising above the roofline. A fireplace would be nice. She enjoyed the warmth and aroma of a wood fire, and Texas winters could be cold.

They drove to the second house on Miranda's list and looked at the exterior, but it was very small and in need of repair, with no central air/heat condenser in the unfenced yard, only a single rusted window unit.

"Cross this one off the list," Emily said.

Miranda called the realtor, Sherry Mason, whose name and phone number she'd jotted down from the "For Sale" sign at the previous house. The woman promised to call back and twenty minutes later she did, arranging to meet them at the Loving house.

It was compact and pleasing to the eye, inside as well as out. There was no updated open concept, the biggest buzz words in the real estate lexicon and the reason few early twentieth-century cottages and bungalows retained their charm and character. This house had both its original design and footprint. The layout was appealing, but cozy, with a wood-burning fireplace in the living room. The two bedrooms were small, but adequate, as was the country style kitchen. To Emily's surprise, a large family room adjoined the kitchen—the house had more square footage than she expected—and it also boasted a fireplace. Sherry said the room was added in the early fifties, years after the house was originally built.

The antique furniture in the living room was beautiful and polished to a glowing sheen, but when the agent noticed Emily eyeing a Chippendale candle stand, she announced briskly that the furniture wouldn't stay with the house. The owner would have it removed when the house sold.

An aging but sturdy stove with four burners and a griddle in the middle of the stovetop stood on one side of the square kitchen, while a refrigerator reminiscent of the sixties was opposite. The mint green appliances were included in the sale price, and Sherry demonstrated their perfect working order in addition to the retro charm they lent the room. A round wooden table surrounded by six ladder-back chairs held pride of place in the center of the room without crowding the space.

"The Lovings built the house in the late forties, and no one else has lived in it," the agent explained. "Miss Rose's husband died when her son was about ten, and she never remarried. The house became known as "Miss Rose's house" and was the most popular meeting place in town for kids. She baked cookies for Garrett's friends who came to visit and held grand birthday parties with performing clowns and pony rides on the lawn.

"Miss Rose loved roses. Well, she'd almost have to with that name, wouldn't she? Those shrub roses on the north side of the house will be full of beautiful pink blooms in the spring because Garrett's kept them pruned."

She motioned toward the back door. "Why don't we step out into the back yard? This way . . ."

She held the door open as Emily and Miranda walked

through and then followed. "This deep porch would be great for relaxing or entertaining. It's large enough for a table and other porch furniture. The big yard has enough room for a garden plot if you're into that sort of thing. Garrett mentioned that his mother planted one every year."

Emily listened to the droning commentary with an occasional nod to show she was attentive, aware that residents of small towns often knew all there was to know about everyone else's lives. She'd grown up in a town about this size, so she was familiar with small town ways. If she moved into this house, no doubt it would continue to be called "Miss Rose's house" for at least ten years, and she would be considered a "newcomer" for the same length of time. Then, again, if Miss Rose was such a beloved figure in this town, the house might always be "Miss Rose's."

Sherry's voice interrupted Emily's thoughts.

"Garrett lives in Dallas, where he owns a commercial real estate company and some other businesses. In addition to this house, he owns several other properties in Cedar Valley. As the only heir of both Miss Rose and her late brother, he was left their family's large land holdings."

The realtor sighed, a sound that caught Emily's attention. Something more interesting than real estate patter might be revealed after all.

"Garrett didn't put this house on the market until three years after his mother died, and you'd think it was a yo-yo the way he's changed his mind repeatedly about selling it. Why, I've shown the property to at least ten couples during the numerous times he's placed it with me over the past three years, but he always finds something he dislikes about the buyers and abruptly pulls it off the market."

The expression on her face revealed her exasperation about that state of affairs before she realized she was revealing too much to a potential buyer. A quick smile morphed her features back into a professional, bland mask.

"However, I think he actually may be ready to sell the house this time. Since he's usually in Dallas, it's probably a lot of trouble for him to hold on to so much personal real estate in Cedar Valley. I heard he's going to sell the other residential properties he owns here, including a huge amount of acreage that belonged to his uncle—all except the ranch, of course. I think he will always hold on to it. If I sell his mother's house, he may let me list the others."

Her brow furrowed and she glanced at Emily, "I had to phone him before I could schedule today's showing. He questioned me extensively about you and your lifestyle before he agreed, but it helped that he knows Miranda and her friend Cassie who cleans the house."

Emily walked back through the rooms alone for another look, amused that her reputation and life had to pass muster with the owner before she could get inside the house.

Homes are bought, not adopted. What's the matter with the man that he keeps sabotaging his chances to sell this house? Since he handles commercial properties, he should know better. I never heard of a seller un-listing a property because of not taking a shine to potential buyers.

She paused in one of the bedrooms and experienced an uncanny sense of warmth not justified by the interior temperature. It settled over her body like a lightweight cloak, and the word *home* suddenly entered Emily's thoughts. The sensation was overwhelmingly strong—a feeling of *déjà vu*—even though she'd never been inside this house before today.

Walking into the larger of the two bedrooms, Emily heard the door behind her slam shut, and a distinct chill replaced the warmth of the connecting room. She turned to see if it was the agent or Miranda who followed her and was surprised to find she was alone. The door she'd left open, however, was closed, and she hadn't imagined the loud bang. Perhaps there was a draft. Emily made a mental note that the windows and doors should be checked for weather-stripping. She opened the door and continued exploring the house.

By the time she looked through all the rooms and walked around the lawns, Emily knew she wanted to buy the property. The size would be adequate for her needs, she liked the layout, and the cottage ambiance appealed to her belief that retro trumped brand-new.

The large family room seemed cozy with its fireplace and window seat, and the covered front porch would make a nice place to meditate and regain her self-confidence. A white wooden-slatted swing at one end of the porch would be the perfect place for her to read in the spring and summer. Besides, sitting in a swing on the front porch was a great way to get to know your neighbors. She felt a longed-for peace as she touched the old sofa and traced her fingers over the redwood window sills.

Yes, she reflected, *this will be my home, my haven, a place where my heart can heal.*

"I want it," she told the realtor. "What's the next step?"

"Are you offering the full price?" At Emily's nod, Sherry said, "I'll start the paperwork when I get back to the office and bring it by for you to sign in about an hour. Are you staying at Miranda's house?"

Emily said she was and gave the agent her cell phone number.

She looked out the window at the neighborhood homes as she rode in the passenger's seat of Miranda's car. The number of large hardwood trees in every yard boded well for a shady street in the spring.

17

Next up, a job, she told herself. Emily expected the local job market to be tight and accepted the prospect of a commute if necessary to find the right job. She didn't want to drive to and from Dallas, but knew she was more likely to find work that matched her skills in one of the larger suburbs. Driving time could be restorative if used to clear her mind of negative thinking or listening to her favorite country music CDs. It would work because she would resolve to make it work. Determination wasn't so difficult when the result affected no one else. That decision brought with it a deeper feeling of calmness than she'd felt even twenty-four hours earlier.

The contract preparation took the realtor longer than her estimate, so Emily and Miranda sat in the kitchen drinking coffee and talking while they waited for Sherry. Miranda told her mother everything she knew about the house's owner, Garrett Loving.

"He's considered quite the catch, both here in Cedar Valley and in the city. Never married, and he has the reputation of a playboy because so many photos of him hit the Dallas paper's society pages. I've seen them. He's always at some swanky event with a different gorgeous woman on his arm. It's rumored he's rolling in money from inheritances on both sides of his family plus his own successful businesses, but he's still down-to-earth enough to spend some weekends on his ranch north of town and can be seen in the hardware store wearing faded jeans and boots.

"I know that for a fact because Jared and I ran into him there when we were renovating this house. He looked like a cowhand buying fence posts—a very
rich cowboy, of course, but authentic nevertheless."

She took a sip of her café au lait. "All the local mothers consider him a saint because he looked after his mother so well when she got older and during her final illness. Nothing was too good for that woman. She had round-the-clock nurses at home instead of regular hospice care. And Garrett took a leave of absence to spend time with her during those last few weeks. He was obviously very close to Miss Rose."

She chuckled. "Of course, the mothers whose daughters set their caps on Garrett as husband material in their teens and got disappointed when he didn't propose felt less kindly toward him and his mother. There were a lot of teary-eyed young things moping around Cedar Valley after he went away to college at the University of North Texas, in Denton.

"After graduation he moved to Dallas, where he has city digs in the penthouse of a plush high rise that was photographed for a glossy decor magazine." Here she raised her arm and wriggled her fingers in the mannerism Emily recognized as sign language for *la-de-dah*. "I don't know anyone who's actually set foot inside his home. It's probably too posh for the likes of us Cedar Valley types who wouldn't know a finger bowl from a cereal dish."

She washed her cup in the sink and set it upside down on the drain board.

"Want a refill, Mom? You don't have to limit your caffeine just because I do. I have a feeling I'll be drinking gallons of coffee to stay awake in a few months, with a baby to care for while trying to squeeze in some writing. I'm stockpiling my rest now while I can."

"Thanks, Mandy. I will have another half cup, no sugar. Now...tell me more about Cedar Valley's ideal of manhood, this Western wonder, Garrett Loving."

"Well, in addition to our casual meet at the hardware store, I've seen him at a couple of town functions, and he's a very charming guy with an old-fashioned gentlemanly manner, almost courtly...the kind of man you see in classic movies. You know—he'll open the door for a woman, stand until she sits, and so forth.

And I must say—he is very good-looking for a guy who's undoubtedly in the neighborhood of fifty. Not that I consider fifty old by any means," she hastily amended with a glance at her mother, who was also nearing that neighborhood.

"If he accepts my offer on the house," Emily said, "I'll get to meet the legendary Mr. Loving at the closing. He will have to be there to sign all the documents unless he has a business manager with authority to do it."

As things turned out, Emily's offer was accepted and the closing was set for two weeks later. Things were moving right along.

Chapter Three

On Saturday before the scheduled meeting to finalize the home sale, the morning dawned clear and mild. Miranda and Emily cleared away breakfast dishes while Jared headed off for a couple of rounds at the golf course.

"Mom," Miranda said as she added the last plate to the dishwasher, "Cassie told me Garrett's having an estate sale at the house today. She said everything of his mother's will be sold except those items he wants to keep for sentimental reasons. Would you like to go over there and see if there's anything you want? I saw you looking at a few pieces while we were there."

"Why not? Yes, I saw some things I liked that would be nice to keep in the house. Let's go."

The street was lined with cars and trucks parked along the curb, so Miranda grabbed a spot that was vacated by a mud-speckled pickup, and the two made their way toward the house that would make Emily Parker the newest resident of Cedar Valley, Texas.

The property sale closing was scheduled for Wednesday morning at an attorney's office in the town square, as she'd been reminded by the real estate agent's call the previous day. The house would be thoroughly cleaned before then, and the lawns would be raked and mulched. Garrett Loving confirmed that the contents would be removed before Wednesday. Emily would receive the keys at the closing and could move in at her convenience.

Emily and Miranda went through the front door and began

looking at the items in the living room that had price tags attached. Most of the heavy antique furniture had *"Not for Sale"* signs, as did the bedroom furniture. Emily wondered why the saintly Mr. Loving hadn't removed everything from the house he didn't plan to sell so as not to confuse or irritate potential buyers. In her opinion, it was a turnoff for customers to see all those things they couldn't buy, but she reminded herself that no one had asked her opinion about the right way to hold an estate sale.

I'll just look around and find things I like that do have price tags. That, and mind my own business.

While Miranda sorted through framed illustrations stacked against the wall looking for something suitable for a nursery, Emily headed for the kitchen to take another look at the kitchen table and chairs. Stepping into the room, she came face to face with a tall attractive man whose Western hat sat at a slight tilt above his tanned face. As they both stopped, he reached up with one hand, removed the hat and gave a slight bow.

"Howdy, ma'am," he said in a leisurely Texas drawl.

Shades of Gary Cooper! Is this guy for real?

The thought blasted into Emily's mind so quickly, she was afraid of having voiced it aloud. Before she had time to recover, Sherry walked up and introduced them.

Garrett replaced his hat, took Emily by the arm and said, "Thank you for your generous offer, Ms. Parker. Please allow me to give you the grand tour of your soon-to-be home."

Emily was speechless, but managed a smile. At this rate, he'd think she was mute. This man was not only handsome, but had the nicest manners of any male she'd encountered in a long time. She felt his warm hand on her arm as he guided her through the house, a house she'd already seen thoroughly, but for which she offered no resistance at seeing again with him. As they walked slowly through the rooms, he kept up a steady narration about growing up in the house. Occasionally, she managed a word or two in response.

They passed through a door into the front hall and almost collided with her daughter.

"Hello, Miranda," Garrett said and tipped his hat. "Been showin' your mom around the house and pointing out some of its characteristics. I think she will be very happy here, and I know Mother would be pleased that such a nice person will be living in the house.

"You know, I didn't change anything after Mother passed until now. It's been hard to drive by the place when I come to town and realize all over again that she's gone. Now, I'll be able to smile whenever I see it, knowing your mom is here taking care of the place. Thank you for telling her about the house. I think it's a good match. Good day, ladies."

With another tip of his hat, he was out the door and gone.

Miranda held up two old-fashioned pastel drawings in matching frames

and asked her mother, "What do you think about these for the nursery? Aren't they adorable?"

Emily nodded, looking a little bemused.

"Mom, are you okay?"

"I'm fine—just surprised to meet Garrett Loving out of the blue, although I should have realized he might attend the sale. I certainly didn't expect him to walk me around the house talking about his boyhood. Everything you said about him is right on the mark, Mandy. He's attractive, charming, and quite the considerate gentleman, which is an exception more than the rule these days.

"I spent the whole time talking to him, so I haven't bought a thing. Let's go see if the kitchen table and chairs are still available."

They were, and Emily was delighted when the SOLD label proclaimed the set as hers. She could envision herself sitting in one of the ladder-back chairs enjoying her morning coffee. She also bought the Chippendale candle stand, aiming a mental *So, there!* at the fussy realtor who'd proclaimed it off limits the previous week. A burgundy cashmere throw that would feel luxurious draped around her while reading completed her purchases.

The meeting at the lawyer's office went smoothly the following week, and a couple of hours later, Emily put her baggage full of clothing and a box of linens into her SUV. A few minutes later, she was opening the door to her new old house. Jared and one of his friends soon arrived with her remaining storage boxes in her son-in-law's truck. While the guys unloaded and placed boxes where Emily directed, the furniture store's delivery truck drove up with the overstuffed sofa and two side chairs she'd bought on sale. It was closely followed by the covered truck manned by two brawny college students hired to bring her Victorian antiques from the Grapevine storage unit.

All the furnishings were in place when Miranda arrived with barbeque in hand from a local take-out eatery, which she served buffet style from the kitchen counter top onto sturdy paper plates. By midnight, a bag of trash smelling faintly of Texas barbecue sauce waited at the curb for garbage pickup.

After her weary helpers left, Emily luxuriated in a long shower, put on warm pajamas and looked around her new domicile once more with pleasure before going to bed. She fell asleep quickly with no awkward first-night-in-a-new-place feeling. When she awoke, it seemed as though she'd lived there a long time. She couldn't recall ever feeling at home so quickly after a move. Like Garrett Loving said, the house was a good match for her.

It was only a week until Thanksgiving, and Emily planned to cook a traditional holiday dinner for her daughter and son-in-law. With the move, grocery shopping and holiday plans occupying her time, she'd given no more thought to Garrett Loving since their handshake at the attorney's office when he signed over to her the deed for Miss Rose's house.

Chapter Four

The cold of the bedroom's oak flooring penetrated Emily's socks, generating another mental note. She needed a warm area rug to place beside her bed. A crackling fire was definitely the order of the day for Thanksgiving, and she was thankful the wood and kindling were already laid, waiting for her to strike a match. Shivering, Emily pulled a bulky blue turtleneck sweater over her head and hoped it would hold in her body warmth.

She watched steam rising from her coffee and thought about the public Thanksgiving service she'd attended with Miranda and Jared at the town community center the previous evening. She'd met a few people at the event whom she would like to know better.

Despite the tendencies of a loner, Emily was determined to meet and mingle with the townspeople of Cedar Valley. She wanted to make new friends and become a real member of the community. Perhaps community participation would get her status as a "newcomer" dropped a few years sooner. Mainly, she intended to keep her mind and body too busy to think about Will or dwell on what she still considered her personal failure.

With Thanksgiving arriving so soon after her move, she'd stored a few unpacked boxes in the spare bedroom and closet. She would have three weeks before Christmas to get everything placed to her satisfaction in order for Miss Rose's house to become "Miss Emily's" home by the big day.

Her coffee cup balanced on the small note pad in her palm, she walked through the house for the third time. She thought it perfect now that her Victorian furnishings graced its rooms. She was thankful she'd left her favorite things behind when moving to

---

the apartment in Kansas. Again, she had the sense of being protected by her subconscious mind in order to safeguard her passed-down-from-generations treasures from her earlier faulty judgment.

God watches out for foolish people too enthralled to see clearly, and for that I'm so thankful.

"Now, how would it look with seating right over there?" Emily spoke aloud as she looked through the window to the back porch where she envisioned a small table and chairs and another swing, with flower pots placed around the perimeter and beside the steps for the summer, and the border flower beds filled with perennials and colorful annuals. Her mind was brimming with plans.

"Miss Rose," she said, "I hope you and I can be friends as I make your lovely house my home."

The spare bedroom made a nice office, while a daybed with trundle tucked beneath it on one side of the room offered sleeping space for overnight guests. She'd thought ahead to the time her as-yet-unborn grandchild was old enough for a sleepover with Grandma. Grammy? Gran? Mmmmm…it was time to start thinking about what she wanted to be called by her grandbaby and any others who followed. Perhaps she should ask Mandy's opinion.

Nothing that sounds like I'm pushing ninety. Certainly not Maw-maw or Granny. I'm happy about becoming a grandmother, but that doesn't mean I want to be "The Beverly Hillbillies" variety.

She watched squirrels scamper up and down the big oak tree just outside a large window in front of which she'd placed her desk, shaking loose the last of the umber leaves that floated to the ground. Turning around, she walked into the hallway of "Miss Emily's" house.

Now, all she needed was to learn of a job opening perfect for her talents. Expenses were low in a small town, so living off savings for quite a while was feasible, but Emily didn't want to use too much of that security cushion. Gainful employment should provide a feeling of stability.

Thanksgiving came and went like the summer breezes she remembered from childhood, with a bounteous dinner at her table enjoyed by Miranda, Jared, and his parents. Lethargic from food, they all adjourned to the family room to watch football on TV, after which Miranda helped her mother with the dishes before she, Jared and his folks went to their house. Emily packed up all the leftovers for them so Miranda wouldn't have to cook.

Another week and November was gone. Time marched on toward Christmas and none too slowly.

Emily spent the first weekend of December decorating the house with garlands, ribbons, ethereal angel figurines, candles in antique holders that had been her mother's, and old-fashioned ornaments she'd inherited. As she coaxed each fragile piece from aging tissue paper and held it up to the light, memories of Christmases from her girlhood through her years as a young wife and mother were kindled to warm her heart. She wanted this Christmas to be special and create new recollections and traditions for her family.

The tree purchased from the town's big box store looked just right in the corner of the room, its tip just beneath the ceiling, and the glow from the strings of retro bubbling lights clipped to its branches made the room seem beautiful and cozy. She loved the overall look that conjured up an earlier era. She'd always been drawn to the look of vintage things, and sentiment played a strong role in her use of Christmas decorations that had been new three generations back.

Coffee mug in hand, she admired the thick garland draped across the fireplace mantel like an inviting forest blanket, small figurines of deer and other animals tucked along its length. She sipped the fragrant brew while she admired her handiwork. Just then she heard a knock on the side door of the family room. Through the small engraved glass window, she saw Garrett Loving waiting on the steps.

"Hello. Come inside," she said warmly as she opened the door.

"This is the first time I've ever had to knock on this door," he said and laughed. "It's kind of a strange feeling."

She smiled and held the door open wide as he walked into the room.

"You're always welcome to drop by for a visit, Mr. Loving. You might want to pull weeds or mow the lawn, so feel free." She laughed recalling the stories he'd told her about the many hours he spent working in the yard for his mother.

"Oh, that's okay. I had my fill of lawn-mowing, but maybe I can recommend a dependable yard service for that." He took off his hat and held it in his hand. "Now, no more of that "Mr. Loving" stuff. That was my father. Call me Garrett because I'm sure we're going to be friends.

"Are you getting everything settled into place? It looks quite lovely in here. I just dropped by to give you the extra set of keys I found in my truck and ask if there is anything else I can do for you. Here's my card. You just call if you need me, okay? I mean it. Don't be bashful."

Handing her the card, he stepped back, tipped the ever-present hat and was out the door before she could say a word. Emily wondered if he really thought her shy. After all, he hadn't given her much opportunity to talk.

She unpacked the remaining boxes and placed the contents in drawers and closets, knowing she would come back after the holiday and rearrange each one. Rubbing an ointment for strained muscles on her aching back would help her sleep. She worked late every night getting the house ready for Christmas because Miranda looked forward to ". . . gathering for Christmas at Mom's house again."

Emily climbed into bed, adjusted her soft pillow, sighed and closed her eyes. Yes, she was home. She drifted into that comfortable limbo state between waking and sleep.

Suddenly, the harsh sound of a door slamming jolted her wide awake and straight into a mind-numbing state of fear. She heard a *thump, thump* that sounded like someone walking in boots, but the sound stopped almost instantly. Was there an intruder? Had someone gotten inside her house after the lights were turned off?

She sat up in bed and spoke loudly while reaching out to the nightstand. She flicked on the lamp, grabbed her cell phone and poised one finger above the number "9."

"What's that? Who's there?"

A frisson of terror danced along her spine as she tiptoed down the hallway turning on the light in every room she passed. Light rid her path of shadows and cast an unnatural glow as she made her way through the house. She called out several times, "Who's there? I've called the police," in a false show of bravado, though her finger hovered above the digit "9" on the phone just in case a 911 call became necessary.

She found nothing, but checked the exterior doors to be certain they were closed and the deadbolts turned to the locked position. All was as it should be.

"Must have been dreaming," she muttered, although she could have sworn the slam that woke her was made by a real wooden door. Shaking her head, she padded back to bed. Satisfied the doors were still locked and no one else was in the house, Emily gradually relaxed, but didn't fall asleep again until the wee hours of the morning. There were no more unexplained sounds to mar the quiet.

Christmas Day dawned overcast and cold. Miranda, Jared and Emily enjoyed the sumptuous luncheon, with its centerpiece the standing rib roast that was their family tradition. There was a lot of laughter, but more than a few yawns. They'd all risen early, and the rich meal made everyone sleepy.

"Let's have a short nap," Miranda said as she sank into the oversized recliner in the family room. "We can open gifts after we've slept off that roast, potatoes and gravy, and, good gracious...way too much dessert. I couldn't stop with just one piece of pie. O-o-oh...I won't need to eat again until after I give birth."

Emily realized her daughter probably needed a nap on a regular basis since she was getting closer to her due date. She remembered that sleeping all night during the third trimester wasn't easy as a baby grew and moved. It was probably easier to doze in a recliner.

"That's a good idea, Mandy—the nap, not fasting until childbirth. I guarantee you'll be hungry again by dinnertime, eating for two. As for napping, I can probably snooze a bit too, and Jared can entertain himself watching Christmas movies on TV."

Miranda looked across the room where her husband's eyes were already closed as he slept sitting upright in an overstuffed chair. She laughed.

"Don't worry about Jared, Mom. He'll be snoring in a minute. The food was delicious, and it was nice to have pepper-rubbed roast the way we did when Daddy was alive. And no one can make pecan pie that tastes like yours. Just wish I hadn't eaten so much. I was already stuffed." She patted her burgeoning belly.

"You've got the house looking great, too, from furnishings

and décor to seasonal decorations. You could be a professional interior decorator, you know?"

She yawned lightly, but her drowsiness appeared to have evaporated. Emily thought that rest in the recliner with her feet propped up would be just as good for Miranda as an actual nap.

"Jared doesn't have to go back to work until after New Year's, and I'm taking a week off from my writing. I've almost finished editing the first volume of my series. I'm going to proof it one more time to be on the safe side before I let go of it and send it to my publisher. Writers are never satisfied, and I'd keep tweaking it for months if I didn't have a deadline. It's time to birth at least one of my babies."

She looked at her mother. "Is there anything you need help with around here, Mom—something that Jared or I can do?"

"I'm good." Emily said smiling. "I only wish I could hear something about a job. I've sent my resume and cover letter to several businesses that have openings matching my experience, but I realize most companies wait until after the new year begins to hire more employees. I'm trying to be patient, never an easy thing for me."

"We can help you pack and store your Christmas decorations whenever you're ready," Miranda said, although she knew Emily liked to leave them in place until after New Year's Day. "Are you as comfortable here as you seem? You do realize you're only the second owner of this house, don't you? That's really unusual in a house of this one's age."

Emily hesitated a moment, but decided to mention the slamming door and the other strange noises she'd heard.

"I've had several weird dreams lately, Mandy, and a couple of days ago, I thought I heard a door slam during the night, followed by a *thump, thump* noise like boots stomping through the house. It woke me, and I searched through all the rooms, but there was nothing there. The doors and windows were all still locked. It must've been a dream—either that, or I've developed a lively pre-slumber imagination.

"I've also had dreams of running through the house with someone chasing me, but I can't see who it is. It brings *The Christmas Carol* movie to mind. I suppose Jacob Marley was in my house the other night with his '*thump, thump.*' I didn't, fortunately, hear the chains," Emily said, laughing at herself.

She didn't mention the colder temperature she sometimes noticed when she walked into her bedroom even though she'd checked the forced-air vent and ensured it was open.

"Well, Mom, stop eating whatever it is you have for a midnight snack before you go to bed. It's obviously interfering with your rest."

And, with that pronouncement, Miranda did doze off, and soon Emily followed suit.

* * *

Snow began to fall on New Year's Day as Jared carried the Christmas tree, undecorated and neatly packed inside its sturdy box, to the storage building. Emily was thankful for the extra storage space, because she enjoyed putting out appropriate decorations on holidays throughout the year. As she walked back toward the house with her son-in-law, the street light cast its glow on a familiar truck parked in her driveway.

Garrett stood in her family room talking to Miranda as Emily and Jared walked in through the back door. The ever-present hat in his hand, Garrett smiled as he handed something to her daughter.

"Well, hello, Garrett. Did you have a pleasant Christmas?"

He looked at Emily and made eye contact. "It was busy. I thought I'd stop by and let you know I hired a chimney sweep to clean the fireplace and check the chimney. We sometimes had chimney sweeps—the birds, that is—build their nests in the spring before I put a screen over the top, and I want to make sure there aren't any stopping up the chimney before you build a fire. I gave Miranda the company's card and wrote my phone number on back, in case you need to call me."

"We built a fire at Thanksgiving and another on Christmas Day, Garrett, and the fireplace worked just fine. There were no critters nesting inside the chimney, and the damper's operable, but thank you for checking. That's very thoughtful of you," Emily said and smiled at him.

"I already paid the man, so you may as well get a free cleaning, unless you'd rather not have him do it. I can call him and say not to come. Just let me know your preference. You have my phone number."

"Thank you, I'll take you up on the cleaning just to be on the safe side. I'll probably build quite a few fires before spring arrives. That's very considerate of you. When's he coming?"

"I told him to give you a call and schedule an appointment. I hope that's okay," he said.

With that, he tipped his hat and backed out the door.

"Do you think he seems uncomfortable in here?" Emily asked as she closed the door behind him.

"I guess it feels strange to visit a house where he grew up and his mother lived the rest of her life now that it belongs to someone else," Jared said. "But he should get used to that after you've lived here for a while."

The young couple left shortly afterward, and Emily tidied up before turning in for the night. Once again she was startled out of sleep by the loud noise that sounded like nothing other than a door slamming. She turned on the bedside lamp and called out again. Searching the house, she found nothing.

It's windy. Maybe I didn't have one of the windows closed all the way and it caused a draft. Or maybe I'm just making up possibilities to avoid being scared.

Emily checked the doors to be sure they were closed securely and locked. She also made certain every window was tightly shut and locked. No means of draft there. She crept back to bed and drifted into an uneasy sleep marred by her recurrent nightmare . . . running and running with someone behind her, *thump, thump.* No rest for the nervous and weary.

* * *

While coffee brewed the next morning, Emily again checked the doors and windows. Everything seemed tight. The window locks were secure.

The dreams must be happening because I'm stressed about finding a job, she reasoned. *Once I'm busy working, they'll stop.*

January neared its end, and Emily still had no job. She was somewhat nervous about her state of unemployment, even though her financial status was positive. It was her nature to be frugal, so she was cautious about expenditures and didn't waste money. She talked daily with Miranda, whose due date was only a few weeks away. It eased Emily's mind that she would be close by to help Miranda when the baby was born.

Chapter Five

It had been years since the late Miss Rose grew vegetables in her garden. Emily couldn't see a reason not to use the same area for her garden, although she wasn't sure where to find someone to till it. She pulled Garrett's business card from her desk drawer and keyed in his phone number, feeling a bit edgy as she heard the ring. She didn't want to impose, but he said to call if she needed anything. She took him at his word.

He must have given her his private number because he answered immediately.

"Hi, Garrett, this is Emily Parker. I hope I'm not encroaching on your schedule, but I want to plant a vegetable garden this spring and need to get the earth tilled before planting time. Do you know anyone in town who would till a spot for me? I thought I'd use the same area your mother used."

"As a matter of fact, I do. Don't worry about it. I'll get someone out there this weekend, if it's okay with you."

"That's great, but please keep in mind that I can't afford to pay a big fee for the work. Perhaps I should get an estimate first."

"How about if I drop by Saturday morning and show you where Mother had her garden?" he asked. "I know someone who is reasonably priced, comes highly recommended, and is very trustworthy."

She agreed and told him goodbye, her nervousness dissipated. He was a nice man and helpful. She tried not to let her thoughts linger on his looks, but instead, to focus on his good qualities. It was impossible, though, to forget how handsome a man Garrett was. She hoped he would come by with the handyman on Saturday. It would be nice to get to know him on a friendlier basis, not just as the former owner of her house.

Emily rose early Saturday morning and dressed for an outdoor work day. She held her usual steaming cup of coffee, from which she was about to take a sip when she heard a knock on the side door. That should be the man who would till a section of the back yard for her garden. She set her cup on the counter, grabbed her jacket and pulled open the door to see Garrett standing on the steps in jeans, boots and a denim jacket. The hole in his right sleeve and the worn corduroy collar indicated that he either borrowed someone's clothes or he was the real deal—not one of those corporate gurus who hired someone to do all physical work for him, but a man who wasn't afraid to get his hands dirty.

"Come in, Garrett. I just poured myself some fresh-brewed coffee. Would you like a cup or perhaps some breakfast?"

"I'll take the coffee," he said, removing his hat and laying it on the table.

Emily caught Garrett watching her intently. As she walked toward him carefully holding the hot coffee, her cheeks grew pink because it was obvious he was looking her over thoroughly. Not in an offensive manner, but appearing genuinely interested in her, the woman. This was not something she'd expected, especially as she wore faded Wranglers and well-worn, but comfortable, scuffed boots with her hair carelessly pulled into a ponytail held by a blue scrunch. Still blushing, she decided to reason this out later . . . not now.

"Garrett, here's your coffee. Where were you just now? Your expression looked as though you were far away from Planet Earth," she said as she set his mug on the kitchen table where he'd probably eaten many meals.

"Oh, I was thinking about your garden. How big you'll want it . . . or maybe I should ask what you're going to plant."

Emily chatted with Garrett about gardening while waiting for the handyman to show up with a tiller. She couldn't help but wonder if Garrett was going to supervise the job or just hang around to make sure the results were to her liking. As she washed their cups at the sink, Emily looked out the kitchen window and saw Garrett's pickup truck, with a tiller in the bed.

Mmmm . . . He must be furnishing the tiller.

Glancing at the clock, Emily commented. "Garrett, don't you think the handyman should be here by now? The morning is getting away from us."

"Oh, uh . . . well . . . , I thought I would till the garden plot for you. That is, if you don't mind. I always did it for Mother, so I've had plenty of practice. If you want, you can use the same plot. The soil's rich and full of loam, and it shouldn't need much in the way of amendments because I've been adding compost to it regularly every year even after Mother was no longer able to work in it. She always wanted me to "get the garden soil ready" even when she couldn't leave her bed, so I did it and just kept on doing it after she passed, simply because I knew how important the garden soil was to her and how she'd want me to take care of it. Does that sound like a silly thing for a grown man to do?" His voice held a hint of embarrassment.

"No, Garrett, I don't find it silly, just the thoughtfulness of a good son who loved his mother. And think how rich and nutrient-filled that garden soil must be by now," she said.

"The plot's right in the center of the back yard where it gets good sun. I always helped her plant and harvest the garden, too. Well, let's say she strongly encouraged me to help out."

He chuckled. "I guess it's handy that she taught me how to garden."

His statement about tilling the garden—before he related his care of the earth during his mother's illness and every year since—finally sunk in, and Emily was struck by a sudden attack of nerves.

"Y—you?" Emily stammered. "You intend to till and plant my garden? I certainly didn't expect you to work in my yard, Garrett. I can afford to pay someone. I just thought . . . when I called you . . . that you would know somebody to hire. I didn't intend for you to do the work."

She knew her words were jumbled together because of anxiety, so she took a deep breath and tried to calm herself before speaking again.

"I'd enjoy helping you put in a garden, Emily. I work on my farm during the summer and feed the livestock in the winter. You see, I'm used to working outside. It's good exercise for staying fit. Besides, I'd like to show you where Mother had her garden."

She gave in gracefully, and they worked together in the back yard for most of the day. Emily pulled weeds and trimmed hedges and tree limbs, as far as she could reach. Dusk set in as Garrett turned off the garden machine, placed his hands on his sides and leaned back to stretch his back muscles.

"Well, what do you think, Emily? Will this spot be big enough for your veggies?"

Emily walked over to stand beside him. She looked up at his face smudged with soil where he'd swiped his hand across his brow and smiled at him.

"Thank you, for giving up your Saturday to work in my back yard. I'll be sure to share whatever yield I get, or maybe I should say whatever we get in our joint garden."

"Thanks. That will be great. Well, it'll be dark soon. I'd best load up the tiller and be on my way. I'm sure you have things to do."

He pushed the machine toward his truck.

"Garrett, why don't you come in and let me fix some dinner

for us in gratitude for all your hard work today. I don't have anything I need to do and, besides, we both have to eat. Come on, you can wash up while I put a meal together. You know your way around here. There are clean towels and soap in the bathroom off the hall."

He nodded and followed Emily into the house. About a half hour later, they sat down to a simple meal of reheated meat loaf (better tasting after it sat in the refrigerator overnight and the flavors "married"), roasted new potatoes, and a crisp salad. Their conversation was easy and enjoyable. He told her about his businesses and the other homes he owned in town that had belonged to members of his extended family, now all gone. She told him about her hunt for a job and how excited she was about her daughter's expected baby. She also mentioned that she'd left Kansas after an unpleasant time there, though she did not add any detail.

"After a year and a half there, I was ready to click my heels and return home to my beloved Texas. I only hope I can find a good job that isn't too far from here, although I don't mind driving if the job pays well, is work I'll enjoy and is challenging."

The evening flew as she began to know him. At one point, he lifted the ladder-back chair in which he'd sat at dinner and showed her the "GL" carved in very small letters near the edge of the bottom slat of the ladder back. It was barely visible since it was covered with several coats of the dark varnish, but he confessed to carving it there with a small pocket knife when he was about eleven to mark it as his seat at the kitchen table. They both laughed when Emily told him he had dibs on that chair any time he ate in her kitchen in the future.

Garrett asked if he could drop by the next weekend to check on her progress. She said that would be okay even though it was a little too early to plant anything. Sometimes an early spring in

Texas got hit by one more frost that killed all the tender young buds and plants. She liked to consult the old-fashioned almanac for farmers before planting.

He thanked her for dinner and left whistling. She grinned as she listened to the cheerful warble while he walked to his truck.

Emily tidied the kitchen and jumped in the shower, anxious to crawl between her warm blankets for a good night's rest. Tired from all the physical work, her muscles sore, it didn't take her long to fall asleep.

Awakened by a door's slam, Emily groaned and got up to search the house. Again, nothing out of the ordinary was visible. She was so tired that she fell back into bed after her investigation and quickly went back to asleep. It was a loud *thump, thump, thump* that next invaded her slumber. A glance at the lighted digital clock numbers told her she'd been asleep for six minutes since the previous rude awakening.

What was that blasted thumping? She switched on the light, and searched throughout the house. Nothing. Mightily annoyed by now, she went back to bed and forced herself to stay awake while she flipped through the pages of a magazine. When thirty minutes passed without sounds, she put the magazine on her bedside table, turned out the light and allowed herself to sleep.

She awoke the next morning with an aching back. Her garden would be worth a little soreness, especially since Garrett helped her and then stayed for supper and an enjoyable conversation. In spite of the interrupted sleep and irritation she'd experienced the night before, she didn't dwell on the bedtime door slamming and thump-thumping noises at all that day. She attended church, spent the afternoon with her daughter and son-in-law and stayed for Jared's specialty barbecued ribs, returned home for an early night and went straight to bed for a peaceful sleep after rubbing liniment on her back.

Emily spent the next week working inside the house—rearranging and adjusting until her furnishings and décor were placed exactly where she wanted them, the parts coalescing into a pleasing whole. It was a comfortable, inviting house and felt more and more like home to her every day. She loved the way every room looked, as well as the porches and the views into both front and back yards. It amazed her that she'd viewed only one house in her search for a home, yet found exactly the one that pleased her as though it had been built to her specifications.

In the evenings she curled up on her overstuffed sofa, spread the soft throw she'd bought at the estate sale of Miss Rose's belongings over her lap and opened the latest Danielle Steele book. The stack of seasoned firewood sent by Garrett was welcome, as was the cleaning the chimney received, courtesy also of the generous Mr. Loving. A crackling fire with red and yellow flames that flickered and darted down to embrace the split wood was warm and relaxing, even though she enjoyed it alone. The aroma of the burning wood and the rhythmic crackling sounds were cathartic.

She was in her usual spot Friday evening, reading in front of the fireplace, when her cell phone rang on the side table. She answered on the second ring.

"Hello, Emily. Garrett Loving, here. Were you sore last weekend after our stint of gardening?"

She loved the sound of his voice. It wasn't Sam Elliot deep, but strong and gentle at the same time. James Garner, she thought, at the age he starred in *Murphy's Law*, just a bit older than Garrett's present age and still a sexy man who won the heart of the younger woman character played by Sally Field...in spite of the self-centered conniving of a younger male character who—come to think of it—reminded her somewhat of Will Forrester.

"Emily? Are you there?"

Garrett's voice drew her back to the present and the phone call.

"I'm here . . . just thinking about one of my favorite old movies. Sorry, Garrett. Yes, my back was sore, but it's better now. In fact, it was a great weekend. With your help, I accomplished quite a few things. I'm glad my garden space is tilled and ready for planting after the last frost."

"Not a problem. I enjoyed the work as well as your company. Oh, and thanks for dinner, which is one of the reasons I'm calling. I'd like to return the treat and take you to dinner tomorrow night if you have no plans. I'll come early so we can discuss what you are going to plant in *our* garden. How about it?"

She agreed, with a strange tug at her heart at the way he spoke of ". . . *our* garden."

43

Chapter Six

When Emily awoke next morning, the first thought that popped into her consciousness was that she had a dinner date with Garrett Loving. She looked forward to the evening, even though she doubted his interest in her was of a romantic nature. He was a well-to-do businessman and reputed playboy whose picture decorated Dallas society pages whenever he escorted beautiful—and no doubt, young—women to fancy parties all over the city. Why would he be interested in a woman near his own age—Emily Parker, a middle-aged woman about to become a first-time grandmother? A fit and attractive, youngish (removed single quotes) grandmother, Mandy would say, but an almost grandmother, nevertheless. He was only treating her to dinner because she'd cooked for him after he helped her prep the garden spot. All the same, she felt excited at the prospect of an evening out with him. She even had nervous flutters.

Stop that, she admonished herself. *There's no reason to get so wound up about dinner in a restaurant with Garrett Loving. It's only a meal and more conversation.*

The morning sun filtered through her bedroom curtains while she dressed for the day in comfortable sweats. She made coffee and sat at the kitchen table with a cup. She'd picked up her organizer to jot down a grocery list when her cell phone's Conway Twitty ringtone sounded.

"Hello, Emily. Already up and finished your morning run?"

By now she'd heard his telephone voice enough that she recognized it without the self-intro—a fact he must also realize since he didn't identify himself.

"Not exactly, Garrett. I'm having my first cup of coffee with my organizer in front of me."

"I'm calling to let you know I'll be in Dallas most of the day. When I leave here, I'll drive straight to your house to pick you up. How does six-ish sound to you?"

"The time is fine," she said. There went that hummingbird flutter in her chest, foolish though it made her feel. Why must she react like a teenager at the thought of an ordinary dinner date?

"Would you like to try that new steak house in Sherman?" he asked. "Sounds great," she replied. "See you at . . . six-ish. I look forward to it."

"Me, too. See you tonight."

Throughout the day, Emily felt her lips curve into a smile whenever she thought about the evening that lay ahead. She wondered if he'd mind her asking questions about his mother and the house he grew up in during dinner. Her curiosity about both Miss Rose and her house's history was growing because of the unexplained door-slamming and thumping. If she told him about the noises, he might think she was crazy. Better stick to general questions about his mother. That would seem natural since she now lived in Miss Rose's house.

The side door squeaked as it opened, and she heard Miranda call out to her, "Mom, are you up?"

"Yes, darling. I'm in the kitchen. Any contractions yet?"

Her daughter's rounded stomach came into view, her face above it wearing a rueful smile. She rubbed her lower back and headed straight for the family room, where she sank into the recliner and raised the footrest. Emily got a tray for her coffee cup, placed a glass of milk on it for Miranda, and then joined her daughter.

"Not a one. In fact, I feel fine, just getting bigger every day. My doctor said he'll do a sonogram on Monday to determine the size of the baby. He told me he may have to induce, but I'm not due for another two weeks. We'll see. Were you busy?"

"Just preparing my to-do list for next week."

Emily paused, her brows knit.

"Listen, Miranda. There's something I want to talk about with you."

"That sure sounds serious, and you look solemn, Mom. Anything wrong?" Miranda shifted her weight in the chair.

"I know it seems ridiculous to even suggest such a thing, but . . . ," and then the words tumbled out of Emily's mouth before she could edit them. "Miranda, I think this house is haunted."

"Haunted? Mom? You've got to be kidding!"

Miranda frowned.

"From the look on your face, you're obviously not kidding, but why on earth would you think that? Here's the most level-headed woman I've known in my life suggesting she now lives in a haunted house. Should we phone for the Ghostbusters?"

"I understand your skepticism, Mandy, but remember when I told you about the doors slamming? It's happened repeatedly since about two weeks after I moved into this house. I've been awakened by slamming doors, but when I get up to check, I don't find anything to explain the loud sounds."

She shook her head as though as surprised at herself as her daughter seemed to be.

"Last Saturday night I heard a "thump, thump," noise that sounded exactly like someone was walking through the house in boots or heavy shoes. It frightened me because I thought someone had broken into the house. I got up, phone in hand ready to call 911, turned on all the lights and looked around, checked the locks—doors and windows—but, again, nothing. It's eerie and unsettling. I've never experienced anything like this before, but I promise you it's happening, and I am not losing my marbles."

Miranda sipped the milk her mother handed her and was quiet for a few moments, thinking. When she spoke, her voice was solemn.

"You remember my friend Cassie who cleaned this house after Miss Rose died? Well, her mom told her stories about Miss Rose and how involved she was in her son's life until he went away to college. She was always a devoted mother, but after her husband died she made Garrett her entire reason for living, not a particularly healthy thing for a mother to do. It must have been emotionally suffocating for him as a boy and young man. Remind me never to do that to my child."

She set her glass on the side table and looked at Emily, her expression pensive.

"Having a mother like that and no father around to temper an atmosphere that must have felt claustrophobic is entirely too much responsibility for a kid to shoulder . . . you know? And it grew worse as he got older. She was the classic over-protective mother. He didn't date much in high school because Miss Rose didn't think any girl was good enough for him. The few girls he dated—the pretty ones who thought they stood a chance with him and hoped for a ring on the third finger, left hand—they couldn't pass her rigid inspection."

She stopped to drain her milk glass, and then continued, "You know how things like that get around in a small town. Even though Garrett was considered a good catch, no mother wants her daughter humiliated, so girls in Cedar Valley started giving him the cold shoulder, even the debutante types.

"Garrett put a stop to that after he left home. He loved his mother and visited her regularly. He made sure she had everything she needed. But no one ever saw him bring a female to this house again."

She giggled. "Several people from town saw him with

47

beautiful women in Dallas, and I've heard it said that a few of them were transplants from Cedar Valley, but it became a matter of pride for the residents to keep it from Miss Rose. Everyone here likes Garrett—he's a super guy—and they respected his mother in spite of her quirky attitude with regard to his love life."

This tidbit of information piqued Emily's curiosity even more about the house's former inhabitant. What it had to do with strange nighttime noises she wasn't sure, but she had the strongest feeling that learning more about Miss Rose might help her unravel the mystery of nocturnal slamming of doors and stomping footsteps.

"What are you doing tonight, Mom?" Miranda asked, lowering the recliner's footrest and edging her awkward midsection closer to the seat's edge. "Jared's planning to grill steaks, and I baked red velvet cake, your fave. Come have dinner with us."

Emily couldn't suppress her sudden smile.

"I have a dinner date tonight with Garrett. He's picking me up at six."

Miranda grinned at her mother.

"Well, how about that? Look at you—dating the most eligible bachelor around. Foxy lady for an almost grandma. Where's he taking you?"

"It really isn't a *date* date, Mandy. He's just paying me back because I made dinner for him last Saturday after he helped me prep the garden spot." She felt her face grow warm beneath a blush. "Still, it's nice to have a friend to share dinner with, and it doesn't hurt that he's a good-looking man."

"Call me tomorrow and let me know how this "friend" date goes for you," Miranda said as she heaved herself out of the chair and waddled toward the door. "I'll be anxious to hear all the details."

The afternoon passed quickly as Emily did chores. Suddenly it was time to get ready for her date. The blue silk shirt she chose matched the irises of her eyes. Black jeans, black shoes and her black leather blazer for the chill in the air completed her outfit. She put on light makeup and small silver eardrops, brushed her shoulder-length fair hair till it shone, and added a spritz of her favorite fragrance. Glancing in the mirror, she liked what she saw. She hoped Garrett would agree.

The chiming of her grandmother's eight-day clock as it started its assent to the six o'clock hour blended with the chiming of the doorbell like a musical scale gliding to its destination. Through the small window in the front door, Emily saw Garrett standing on the porch, the tops of colorful flowers and greenery visible just beneath his chin. How thoughtful of him to bring flowers!

As she watched, he smiled and waved to a passerby. Of course, everyone in town knew him. Now they would also know he visited her bringing flowers. By tomorrow night, there might be talk of their engagement. Such was the small town rumor mill. Emily smiled at the vagaries of Cedar Valley, her new small town home.

She opened the door and said, "Come in, Garrett. You look nice."

His starched jeans had a very straight crease down each leg. The corduroy jacket he wore was the same color as the curls freed from the western hat he now held so politely in his hand. Ostrich-skin boots completed his authentic western look.

Does he dress in western attire for business? She couldn't help but wonder this, since he'd come straight to her house from a workday in Dallas.

Garrett handed her the bouquet of mixed flowers, their stems wrapped with tissue paper and tied with a narrow pink ribbon. "I thought you might like spring flowers. I know you're as ready for warmer weather as I am. You look wonderful."

He smiled, and his eyes caught the soft light from the old-fashioned chandelier. "By the way, that blouse is the same color as your eyes."

"Thank you, Garrett. Your own eyes are what I call that special Paul Newman shade of blue. I'll bet they pick up the color of a blue shirt when you wear one, don't they?"

He looked down with a shy smile at her compliment, though he didn't strike her as reserved. Besides, she felt certain he heard everything from sincere praise to sheer flattery from other women all the time. What a strange reaction.

He opened the front door for her, waited as she locked it, and placed his hand on her elbow as he walked her to his waiting red Cadillac.

Aha, so we aren't traveling in the truck this evening. I am impressed.

Ever the gentleman, he opened her door and held it for her while she slid onto her seat. The passenger's seat was covered in luxurious soft leather the color of cream. She watched him walk around to the driver's door, his hat set slightly back on his head. She silently chided herself for staring as she buckled her seat belt.

This is only a friendly pay-back meal, nothing more. Don't think about his looks. Concentrate on his personality, his friendly behavior. He's just a nice guy.

In spite of the little pep talk she gave herself, Emily couldn't remove her eyes from Garrett's lean frame and had to struggle to keep a straight face when he got into the car.

He slid effortlessly into the driver's seat and started the engine. She watched his shapely hands caress the leather-wrapped steering wheel as he peered into the rearview mirror and backed the car out of her driveway.

50

"Heard anything about a job yet?" His tone conveyed real interest. She didn't think he was simply making small talk.

"Nothing so far, but I'm hoping companies begin ramping up their workforce for the new season and have openings."

"I have a lot of contacts in the business world, both in Dallas and in the larger suburbs close to Cedar Valley. I'll check on openings. Didn't Miranda tell me your background is in marketing?"

She chatted about her previous jobs and the variety of work she did while Garrett drove to a restaurant located in a remote area slightly north of Sherman. Inside, Emily was enchanted by its rustic ambiance. The tables and chairs looked as though they were fashioned from freshly-cut trees, with twigs curling in random places. There was even real sawdust on the floor, but the wood beneath it gleamed. The host showed them to a table in the back of the room where it was quiet enough for conversation. Emily hoped she could find an unobtrusive way to bring up the topic of Miss Rose as they talked over dinner.

The lighting was dim, and she had difficulty reading the menu. Either Garrett had already been here before, or he automatically ordered steak with all the fixings wherever he dined. Emily chose a light fish dinner seasoned with herbs and lemon. Appetizers of pita wedges with hot spinach dip stimulated her appetite, and she enjoyed the entrée that followed. Crème Brule and coffee made the perfect ending.

Emily was bolstering her courage to tell Garrett about the strange noises in her house when he asked, "Have you decided what to plant in the garden?"

"Well, I . . . ,"

She was interrupted by the vibration of her cell phone. She saw her son-in-law's name on the display and felt a vague unease. It was unusual for him to call her instead of Miranda.

"Excuse me, Garrett, but I need to get this. It's Jared. Miranda might be in labor."

She answered the phone to learn they were indeed at the hospital. Jared told her Miranda fell down the steps from the kitchen. Contractions began almost immediately, so he rushed her to the hospital. The doctor was examining her as he spoke.

Chapter Seven

"Garrett, I need to go," Emily said when the call ended. "Miranda took a tumble that started premature labor. She's at the hospital, and I need to go to her. I don't know if she's badly injured or anything about the baby's condition. Jared's waiting to talk to her doctor."

Garrett saw the worry in her eyes and assured her they would get to the hospital quickly. A few minutes later they were in the car headed for the Whitesboro medical center. Garrett talked calmly in an effort to distract Emily from imagining the worst, but she didn't really hear him.

Fearsome scenarios raced through her mind. What if something terrible happened to the baby? To Miranda? Although she heard the Caddy's engine purring, they seemed to be traveling in slow motion. The cars in front of them crept along, and they caught every red light on the way. She thought about the very pregnant Miranda falling down her concrete back steps, and her heart caught in her throat. Tears stung her eyes as she worried about her daughter and the baby so close to life whose wellbeing might now be precarious.

Garrett saw her fear and reached for her hand in reassurance. She looked up at him and forced a small smile. He was a secure and comforting man to have beside her in a frightening situation.

Finally! The neon sign, "EMERGENCY ROOM", glowed just ahead, and Garrett pulled into the parking bay nearest the double doors.

The emergency room wasn't crowded, and Emily hoped that meant Miranda would get fast attention. She was asking a nurse at the desk where to find Miranda when she heard her name. Turning, she saw Jared hurrying toward them down the hall. He hugged Emily and then described the accident.

While he started a fire in the grill, Miranda hosed off the driveway, patio, and concrete steps. She was taking the steaks out to the patio when she slipped on the slick wet steps and fell. He heard her scream from the kitchen where he was gathering his grilling tools and rushed outside. A freak accident like that would be bad at any time, but with Miranda heavily pregnant . . . He covered his face with his hands and Emily hugged him.

"I'd better get back in there with her," he said. "They won't let anyone else go in right now, but I'll let you know as soon as I have anything to report."

"Kiss her and tell her I love her, Jared, and I can't wait to see that new baby girl or boy," she told him as she felt Garrett's warm arm slip around her shoulders.

Leaning against him, her energy sapped by tension, she realized nothing had made her feel more secure than his arm in a very long time. He led her to a row of blue and yellow chairs on the other side of the waiting room. As they sat, she noticed the nurses at the ER desk looking their way. *Checking out Garrett,* she thought. *He must get lots of attention.* But that was the least of her concerns right now.

Emily felt as though the tortoise and the hare were in the waiting room that night. She was the hare, wanting to get to the finish line, and Father Time was the tortoise, holding everything back. It was a nerve-wracking situation, with no clue to the outcome.

Garrett found a coffee machine and fetched cups of its tasteless lukewarm brew several times during the long night. At least it had the jolt of caffeine. Periodically, Emily walked to the desk and asked the nurses if there was any news about Miranda, but each time she was told they hadn't heard anything. Resting her head on Garrett's shoulder with his arm around her, praying that no news was a good sign, she waited with him mostly in a silence broken only by the ringing of the ER phones and the soft swishing sounds of rubber-soled shoes as doctors and nurses came and went.

Emily dozed off and felt herself running from something . . . a nameless whatever that shoved her. She woke with a start and noticed the large wall clock. It was four o'clock in the morning. How long had she been asleep? When her eyes focused, a man in white scrubs was walking up to her. He introduced himself as Miranda's doctor.

"How is my daughter?" she asked. "Is the baby okay?"

"They're both fine, Ms. Parker. We had a tough go for a while, but everything's all right now. I'll let her husband tell you about the baby when he comes out. Dads always want to deliver that news. We doctors just deliver the babies."

He chuckled, a sound Emily found reassuring. "The nurses will be taking care of Miranda for a bit. Then you can see her."

Emily breathed a big sigh of relief as he walked away. Miranda was okay, and so was her baby.

I have a brand new granddaughter or grandson—did the doctor say which? It doesn't matter, as long as both the baby and Miranda are safe and healthy.

"Congratulations, Grandma," Garrett said as he hugged her. He followed the hug with a kiss on the cheek.

"Looks like you're going to be busy for a while with a new baby in the family. I just hope you'll save a little bit of your spare time for me."

"Garrett, thank you so much for driving me here and staying to keep me company. I would have been a nervous wreck trying to get here and waiting all alone. But I've taken up your entire night, and I'm sure you're ready for some rest. Don't worry about seeing me home. I can catch a ride with Jared after I see Miranda and the baby. Oh . . . , and thank you for a wonderful dinner. I enjoyed every moment of it right up to that emergency phone call."

Just then Jared walked through the double doors into the waiting room with a Texas-size smile spread across his face.

"We have a boy, Em! Seven pounds, six ounces and twenty-one inches long, and he was yelling bloody murder when I left Miranda's room."

"How's Mandy?" Emily asked.

"She's doing great now and wants to see you."

Jared motioned for Emily to follow him down the hall. She glanced back at Garrett, smiled and waved at him before she left.

Emily entered her daughter's room and saw her propped up in bed holding the baby. *What a beautiful sight. My baby girl just gave birth to a baby boy, and here they are, both okay. It doesn't get much better than this.*

She leaned down to hug her daughter and kiss her newborn grandson on his soft little head covered in sparse hair that looked like dark peach fuzz.

Miranda was a bit hyper, evident in her rapid speech.

"Isn't he just the cutest little thing you've ever seen, Mom? Look at his little fingers and toes. See his adorable tiny ears that look like seashells and those precious lips shaped like a rose bud? Mom, we're going to name him Christopher Austin after Dad. I think he would like that, don't you?"

"I know he would like that, Mandy. I'll bet your dad's beaming somewhere in heaven about his new grandson and proud to have him as a namesake."

Emily wiped away a tear before it could slide down her cheek. It didn't seem possible Miranda's dad had been gone

---

56

almost seven years. She had barely been able to function in her grief during that first year after his sudden death. She still missed him, and if she probed the nearly healed emotional scar too strongly, it still hurt, but it was easier now to remember the good times. She was happy this new little guy would carry his name.

When Emily walked back to the waiting room, she saw Garrett still sitting in the same chair grinning at her.

"I thought you'd be gone," she said, sinking into the chair beside him.

"Nope. I'm waiting to take you home or to breakfast, whichever you choose, or we can do both. How about breakfast first, and then I can drive you home? Besides, I want to take a look at your garden, and we didn't get to have our discussion about what to plant."

She nodded as he took her hand, and they walked out of the building to his car.

Chapter Eight

"What a night! Let me make us some breakfast. I want some real coffee, don't you, after that tepid colored water at the hospital? Now that I'm relieved about Miranda and the baby, I'm hungry, too."

Emily unlocked the door to her house and invited him inside. They'd stopped at the local book store/café Haus on the square in town, but it wasn't yet open.

They worked in tandem in her kitchen, Garrett making the coffee while she warmed cinnamon buns in the microwave and scrambled eggs. As she put the food on plates, she smiled at him.

"I really do appreciate your staying at the hospital with me, Garrett. I'll bet you didn't expect to spend the night waiting for a baby to be born when you picked me up for dinner at six-ish last evening."

Garrett raised a mug to his lips and drank a cautious sip. He smiled at her with genuine warmth.

"I didn't mind it at all. I've never waited for a baby's birth before. The circumstances were worrisome, but it gave us more time together, Emily, and I liked watching you sleep curled up next to me. I even enjoyed hearing you purr a little while you slept. And everything was great when we found out that both Miranda and the baby were okay. That was worth waiting for, you know."

"Purr? You mean...I snored? How embarrassing. Why didn't you wake me?"

"It was just a little purring, like a kitten. No big deal. I'm sure I snored like a freight train. Don't most men?"

She was perplexed as she poured herself a cup of coffee and

topped off his cup.

"I didn't even know you went to sleep, but I was too knocked out to hear you snore. Um, this is good coffee, not too strong and very tasty. Can you by any chance cook as well?"

They continued the small talk for a while, exchanging more tidbits and learning more about each other. She discovered he liked to fish and had a pond stocked with bass on his farm. It was easier, he said, to catch them in a smaller area, and he mostly did it for the sport, although sometimes he did clean and cook them on his grill. He invited Emily to his farm for fishing and grilling. He would also give her a tour of the ranch. The invitation was open-ended, ". . . whenever you have time on a weekend this spring."

She asked him about growing up in a small town and about his mother, and then just sat back and let him talk.

He said Miss Rose took him to Sunday school every week when he was a boy and encouraged him to attend church camps each summer, which he enjoyed. He told Emily he knew it was a sad day for his mother when he graduated from high school and went away to college. He worried about leaving her alone since his dad had passed away when he was only ten and left him to become the man of the family. He knew his mother depended on him.

He told her how devastated his mother was when he chose to live in Dallas instead of coming back to his hometown after earning his degree. He hoped she ultimately understood that he couldn't develop the kind of business interests in a small town that were possible in a large city. He'd visited her regularly, so he hoped she didn't feel abandoned.

"I suggested buying an apartment for her near me in the city, but she wouldn't hear of it. Mother grew up in Cedar Valley and never liked Dallas or any other city. She would have been miserable away from this small town, so I didn't press her.

Instead, I came to visit and allowed her to spoil me with her cooking while I was here. I coaxed her out to the ranch occasionally, but that place had been Dad's bailiwick, and I think she considered it a male domain, not ladylike enough for her. Mother was a bit old-fashioned, you may have gathered by now."

Emily told him of her love for books and that she wrote poetry. Her hope was to one day become a published writer like her daughter. She said she dreamed of their collaboration as a mother-and-daughter writing team. She reassured him that she wasn't nerdy—she just enjoyed writing and liked to read fiction of almost any genre.

She also described her own childhood, growing up in Grapevine when it was still a small town with Longhorns grazing behind fences out on the highway. Now it was a burgeoning suburb that was barely recognizable, but she missed its former small town essence and was happy to adopt Cedar Valley as her new home.

Glancing at the clock, she couldn't believe they'd been exchanging stories for three hours. It was already noon.

"Garrett, it's the middle of the day. Do you want to take a look at the garden spot now?"

They walked through the family room and out into the back yard. He grabbed his hat on the way out and, brushing back his dark curls, pushed the hat onto his head. She liked the hat, and she liked him, though not in that order. It had rained on the spot he tilled, and he thought it might need to be tilled one more time since it would soon be time to begin putting plants in the ground.

He told Emily he would come back the next Saturday and turn the soil one more time so it would be ready to plant after the last frost of the season. Walking around the house to where he'd left the Caddy, he caught Emily's hand and held it snugly in his larger one.

"Thank you again for staying at the hospital with me last night," she said. "It was very comforting having you there. I'll be sure to let Miranda know you stayed with me and were concerned about her."

"Any time, Emily. Tell Miranda I hope she and her new son get along okay and get to go home soon. I'll see you next Saturday."

And with that, he reached down and kissed her with soft full lips, pushed back his hat, began to whistle and was in the car and gone before Emily could recover. Her heart pounded as she touched her lips with her fingers and watched the red car move down the street.

Emily drove to the hospital in the afternoon to see her daughter and new grandson. They both looked great when she walked into the room. She leaned over and planted a kiss on her daughter's cheek and one on the boy's soft little head.

"Mandy, I can't believe how great you look after your ordeal. You don't look like you just had a baby, except, of course, that you're much thinner. And Christopher Austin is all dressed up in his blue onesie that just fits. What a handsome young man he is. By the way, what are you going to call him . . . as an everyday name, I mean? Christopher Austin is quite a mouthful."

Miranda was calm. "We're calling him Chris. Oh, we're both just fine, Mom. Thanks for staying last night. I didn't want Jared to call you, but it soon became evident little Chris decided it was time to enter the world. I was afraid they wouldn't let Jared stay with me after I had the accident, and I was so relieved he could.

"Gee, I'm sorry you had to stay in that crummy waiting room alone so long, but they wouldn't allow anyone other than Jared to be in the room with me. I hope you found something to read."

"I wasn't alone," Emily told her daughter, not trying to hold back her smile. "Garrett drove me from the restaurant after Jared called, and he stayed in the waiting room with me all night. He drove me back to Cedar Valley after I saw you early this morning. We had breakfast at my house and talked for hours. He's such a nice man, Mandy."

"Well, now, isn't that interesting? He tills your garden, takes you to dinner and stays with you in an all-nighter waiting for a grandbaby to be born. What's going on here, Mom? This sounds serious. Don't tell me you've nabbed the most eligible bachelor in Cedar Valley! Seriously, he is a nice man, and you could do worse. Pardon me for saying it, but you may need a reminder that you have done worse and are still recovering from that decision. Just be careful—that's all I ask. It may only be rumor, but I hear Garrett Loving plays the field a lot and dates many different women in Dallas. I don't want you to get hurt . . . again."

Emily assured her daughter that Garrett was just a friend. It didn't seem the right time to mention his invitation to catch fish at his ranch that he would grill for dinner and then take her on a tour of the property.

Besides, he was vague about the invitation. Sometime this spring? He was only trying to be nice and, besides, I think it might be hard for him to let go of his mother's house emotionally. That's probably the reason he is being so helpful with everything. Of course, that has no bearing on the soulful kiss he gave me before he left. Mmmmm . . .

She held her little grandson for a while, marveling at his perfect little features. Healthy babies were flawless specimens of the human race, nothing yet to mar their baby bodies or baby minds, and Emily was so glad baby Chris was healthy. She kissed his tiny cheek before she gave him back to Miranda, kissed her daughter goodbye and drove the short distance from the hospital to her home.

She liked thinking of the house and grounds as *my home*. It was still early evening when she arrived, so she decided to sit on the back porch and read a while before turning in for the night. In spite of only having a brief nap in a hospital waiting room chair the night before, she felt strangely exhilarated. Maybe that's how becoming a grandmother affected one.

She was glad the days were getting longer because the extra sunlight would allow her more time to work in the yard. A trip to the plant nursery was on her agenda for the following week. Garrett would till the plot one more time so she could plant her favorite vegetables for the summer garden. She was busy making a list for her garden and things she needed to do for the week when she heard her cell phone ring in the house where she'd left it. She hurried inside to answer. It was Garrett.

"I wanted to catch you before you turned in for the night to tell you to have a great week," he said softly, "and to tell you I had a great time with you, especially at your house for breakfast. I'm glad everything's okay with Miranda and the baby."

"Thanks Garrett, and again, thank you for staying at the hospital with me last night."

"I'll see you next weekend."

She heard the click.

That night Emily was wakened from deep REM sleep by the loud bang as a door slammed. She jumped out of bed and switched on the light. Searching through the house, she couldn't figure out which door she had heard because she felt disoriented. What difference did it make anyway which one was slammed? Just the fact that the slam happened at all was stressful enough. Emily was getting tired of this nighttime routine. It was the only thing that marred the happiness she felt in her new home.

Getting back into bed, she switched off the lamp and settled down again. Soon she drifted back to sleep, and the rest of the night was peaceful. She even slept in the next morning to catch up on slumber lost the previous night. She enjoyed brunch in a relaxed, happy mood.

Her son-in-law phoned on Monday to say he would bring Miranda and their new baby home Wednesday afternoon. Emily told him she'd freshen up the house and cook dinner for them. At midday, she walked over to their house to make certain everything was ready for their arrival. She put dinner in the oven, changed the sheets on the master bed for Miranda and put sheets on the baby bed that, fortunately, Jared had assembled weeks ago.

Emily hummed as she checked the doneness of the pot roast. She hoped Jared would like the tender potatoes and carrots she'd placed around it. She didn't add much seasoning or any onions since her daughter would be breastfeeding the baby.

Life is good, Emily thought as she heard the car in the driveway.

The afternoon passed quickly as she helped her daughter and grandson get settled in. Jared invited her to stay for an early dinner, and she cleaned up the kitchen afterward. She told Miranda she would be back the next morning to lend a hand with the baby since Jared was going back to work. She would love spending time with them. Jared had always been nice to her and was good to her daughter. The couple loved each other deeply, and now their family was blessed with a beautiful baby boy. Yes, life was certainly good. In fact, it was pretty near perfect.

She walked the short distance back to her home. It was close to sundown, but she felt safe walking by the small retail shops around the square. The coffee shop would be a great place to visit. A notice posted on the bulletin board of the coffee shop announced a group of writers met there two times a month. That would be nice to drop in on some time, and she knew there was a consignment store with lots of handmade items for sale, and of course, there was the local newspaper office, the letters of *The Tribune* barely legible across the faded sign.

Arriving home, she walked into her house and switched on a light in the kitchen, just as her cell phone vibrated in her pocket. She'd turned off the sound while at her daughter's to avoid waking the baby. Not expecting anyone, she was surprised to see Garrett's number on the Caller ID.

"Hello, Garrett. I just walked in the door from Mandy's. I walked around the town square before I came home."

"I called to remind you that I'm coming Saturday morning to till the garden again. Should I pick up seeds or flats of seedlings this week?"

"Thanks anyway, but I have that on my agenda. I plan to get some potatoes, broccoli, cauliflower and lettuce, and—oh yes— spring onions to plant for now. When it gets warmer, I'll add tomatoes and spinach. How does that sound?"

"Like a good salad," he said with a chuckle. "Are you sure you don't want me to pick up things and save you the bother?"

"Thanks, but I can get them tomorrow or Friday."

Emily wondered why he kept offering to run errands for her when she felt certain his business days in Dallas didn't leave time for garden shopping.

"Emily, I really just wanted to talk to you tonight. I wanted to hear your voice. Do you realize I am smitten with you? I love being around you. I love the way you take care of your family and the way you take care of Mother's house . . . I mean, your house, but it means a lot to me to see the love you put into it. I feel at home when I'm visiting you just as I did when I lived there.

"I find myself thinking about you during the day, wondering where you are in the house, and thinking about how you looked and felt as you leaned against me in the hospital. So there, I said it. I hope I don't scare you off or offend you by my words, but you, Emily Parker, have turned my world upside down, and I couldn't go another day without telling you."

Emily didn't say anything because her heart pounded so loudly she could hear the heartbeat in her ears, and she had trouble breathing. She was astonished by Garrett's declaration and afraid she might hyperventilate at any moment. The most eligible bachelor in town—this gorgeous hunky man—told her he'd fallen for her.

Emily had never thought of herself as beautiful. People had called her pretty all of her life, but surely there were many truly gorgeous women in Garrett's life in Dallas . . . women he saw frequently . . . women photographed by paparazzi. Surely he didn't prefer pretty little Emily Parker over them. Did he?

Garrett asked in a quiet voice, "Emily, are you there?"

"Yes, I'm here, Garrett," she said, wondering if he regretted what he'd blurted out a moment earlier. "I don't know what to say. Of course, I'm attracted to you. Who isn't? I understand you have a lot of beautiful girls in Dallas standing in line for you.

"I need to explain something to you to explain why I seem hesitant. I was in a really bad relationship before I moved here, and the breakup was messy and traumatic. I'm afraid of moving too quickly into a rebound relationship and having it end badly if I don't take the necessary time to get to know someone before making any kind of commitment. I learned a lot the hard way from my bad experience, and the whole point of such a lesson is to avoid making the same mistakes again. I don't have all the answers, Garrett, but I do know I never want to be in a miserable situation again."

She paused for a moment and her tone softened. "I hope I don't offend you by telling you all this, Garrett. Thank you for the compliments you paid me. I feel honored that you consider me special. I'll see you Saturday if you still want to help me with the garden."

She waited in the quiet stillness for his response.

When he spoke, his voice was calm and even. "I understand what you're saying, Emily. I'm in no hurry. I just want to keep seeing you and getting to know you. Hopefully, you'll want to know me, and, yes, I want to continue helping with the garden. I'm sorry if I spoke too soon. I don't want you to feel pressured. You're doing great. Maybe one of these days, you'll be able to share with me the things that trouble you about relationships, but I want you to know that I intend to pursue you until you tell me to go. So, for now, I'll say good night and that I'll see you Saturday morning."

Emily heard the click but didn't immediately disconnect her phone. She sat there pondering his words.

Smitten. Did he really say smitten? Who uses the word smitten these days? Turned my world upside down. Fallen for you. Did he say all those things? Yes, he did. I heard him say them. He said them to me. Me, Emily Parker.

She was attracted to Garrett and felt drawn to him each time they were together. It was true that she felt very close to him, but he'd said that he had fallen for her. That phrase was a little frightening. It was too reminiscent of the things Will said to her in the early days of their relationship.

As she prepared for bed, his words raced through her mind like a thoroughbred horse rounding the turn to the finish line. Pulling the covers up to her chin, she smiled and heard faint echoes of Garrett's strong yet gentle voice saying "smitten", "turned my world upside down" and "I've fallen for you" as she drifted off to sleep.

Bam!

Somewhere a door slammed hard, as though an angry person wanted to break it off its hinges. Emily, startled and irritated, jumped out of bed and switched on the bedroom light. For some reason, she looked up at the ceiling.

"Okay, whoever you are, come on out and show yourself instead of slamming doors! Is that you, Miss Rose? Are you trying to tell me something? Why do you only slam the doors when I've been with or talked to Garrett? I know you think he's your little boy, but he's also a grown man who can make his own decisions. Now, leave me alone."

With that, she crawled back into bed and switched off the light. She didn't hear the door slam again that night.

Thinking of the situation over coffee the next morning, she wondered if Garrett's mother didn't want him to come to this house to see her.

Or, is it that she doesn't want me living in her house?

Should she tell Garrett? Maybe not, maybe since she had confronted . . . what? Exactly what . . . or who . . . had she confronted last night? Was it the ghost of Miss Rose? Would that specter leave her alone now that she had spoken her mind?

Emily thought it best to wait and see if there was any more ghostly activity again before mentioning the issue to Garrett. After all, he would be there on Saturday, and the manifestations occurred after he was with Emily or talked to her on the phone. She decided to wait until after Saturday to see what happened before saying anything to him. After all, she was about to suggest to a man she admired that his beloved late mother might be a ghost.

Chapter Nine

Emily chose a variety of vegetable plants in various stages at the nursery on Friday, eager to begin her garden now that they'd likely seen the last frost of the season. After dinner she sat in a new wicker chair on her back porch, looked over the big yard and admired the stirring signs of spring, the green buds on all the trees and sprigs of bright green grass poking up from the ground around the garden plot. Peace and contentment warmed her like rays from the March sun.

The elements of her life that mattered had finally come together. She loved her house and the feeling it gave her that she'd found a home. Her daughter had a new baby boy, a sweet grandson Emily would have the joy of watching grow into a boy and, eventually, become a man.

Added to these blessings, she may have met someone with whom she could become close despite Miranda's warnings. ("Be careful, Mom. He has a reputation as a playboy, and I don't want you to get hurt again.")

Emily leaned back in her chair and closed her eyes, recalling her last conversation with Garrett. He'd admitted to strong feelings for her and said he would act on those feelings until the time she told him to go. He . . .

"Hello! Anyone home?"

Emily opened her eyes. Garrett stood on the porch steps nearly in front of her chair. She hadn't heard him open the gate to the back yard. Struggling to tear her thoughts away from the words he'd said last night and focus instead on the present was difficult to do quickly.

"I hope I didn't startle you, Emily. I'm on my way to the ranch and thought I'd stop by to say hello."

"No, Garrett, I was just making a mental note of the types of container plants I want to place around the porch and some annuals I'd like to add to the flower beds. Would you like to come in for a cup of coffee?"

She rose from the chair and stepped past him as he held the door for her, feeling the response of her blush warm beneath his kiss on her cheek. Not only was her face turning pink, there went that crazy drum beating inside her chest. She was sure he must hear it over the squeak of the back door.

"I must spray some oil on those hinges," she said to cover whatever sound was audible.

"Did you get plants for the garden yet? I drove in tonight so we can get an early morning start." At her nod, he asked, "What kind did you select?"

"They're in the storage shed, Garrett. Want to take a look at them? Let me get a jacket."

She walked toward her bedroom and heard footsteps behind her. Not again with the footsteps. Not now. She whirled around and was cheek to chest with Garrett. How tall he was! Her breath grew ragged as she looked into his face just as he pulled her into his arms and covered her lips with his own. The kiss was warm and passionate, nothing she could describe as friendly.

Were they in a room inside a house, or were they on a beach with waves crashing over them? Emily's sense of her surroundings was indistinct and became even more confused as his lips pressed against her own and his arms encircled her.

Bam! The door behind them slammed shut. Emily pulled away from Garrett and turned toward the door.

Garrett looked at her. "What was that?"

Her words rushed out much as they'd done when she talked to Miranda about the phenomenon.

"This is something I've wanted to talk to you about, Garrett. Since the second week I moved into this house, I've been awakened by a door slamming, and it only happens when you've been here or I've talked to you on the phone. Actually, it began the day you showed me around the house. I know this sounds crazy, but I think the doors are being slammed by your mother."

Garrett took her by the arms, led her to the bed and sat beside her there. He said in a very calm voice, as though talking to a slightly hysterical child,

"Emily, my mother has been dead for six years. I lived in this house from birth until I went to college, and I never heard anything like that. I haven't heard doors slam since my mother's death, either, and I checked the place regularly for six years. Are you sure you weren't dreaming?"

"So now you think I'm hearing things? That it's my imagination? Even though you heard the door slam just now? You heard it too, didn't you? At least, I remember you asking what it was."

Her frustration was unmistakable, making her voice rise in tone.

"I didn't mean that I thought you were imagining anything, Emily. Yes, I heard the door slam, but maybe it was caused by wind blowing through the house, or perhaps you didn't have the door closed tightly, and a sudden draft made it slam."

Folding her arms, Emily frowned and shook her head. He didn't believe her. Why bother saying anything else if he thought she had a wild imagination? Grabbing her jacket, Emily reached for the door knob and said, "Let's go to the storage building."

She twisted and pulled on the door, but nothing happened.

"I . . . can't . . . open . . . this . . . door."

"The house must have settled and made the door unlevel. These old houses sometimes do that. It's probably just stuck."

71

Emily watched as he reached for the knob and pulled the door. It opened easily. There was a squeak as he pushed the door back until it touched the wall. She wrapped her arms around her shoulders as if to ward off the flush of indignation spreading throughout her body.

Great, she thought, *the door opens for him as easy as pie. Now he certainly won't believe anything I say about the doors slamming or the possibility that his mother's haunting my house. I may as well keep my thoughts to myself about that little matter.*

"The door looks all right to me, Emily. So, you think Miss Rose either doesn't want you in her house or doesn't want me with you in her house?"

She answered him slowly, unconsciously mimicking his earlier manner of explaining something to a truculent child.

"Garrett, I simply know that every time you're here, I hear a door slam during the night, but when I get up to check, I don't find anything. It's happened repeatedly. I rarely get an undisturbed night of sleep. Oh, yes, there's a thumping sound, too, like boots stomping across the floor."

"And you're sure you left the doors open?"

"Wasn't this door open when we came into the room?"

She saw him hesitate, but then he took her by the hand. He led her into the kitchen and pulled out one of the chairs for her to sit. He brought her a glass of water and then sat in a chair that he pulled up close to her. Holding both of her hands, he looked at her and sighed, a look of resignation settling into his eyes and across his face.

"Emily, there's something I need to explain to you about my mother. Something I've only admitted to myself until now."

Chapter Ten

Emily's heart fluttered and her pulse quickened as she looked into Garrett's eyes.

What is it?

She willed him to tell her whatever it was about his mother that he'd never told anyone before, and his long sigh only heightened her anxiety. Whatever it was, she needed to know the truth. What was it about Miss Rose that made him sigh that way?

"When I was a boy growing up in this house—"

The front doorbell rang with three long peals, communicating the impatience of someone who didn't want to be kept waiting. Emily flinched at the strident rings.

"No one ever uses the bell," she said, reluctantly freeing her hands from the comfort of his warm ones. "I'd better see who it is."

She opened the front door and recoiled at the sight of Will Forrester standing on her porch, his thumbs curled through the belt loops of his jeans. It was a familiar pose he used because he thought it made him appear in control.

"Will! Wh—what are you doing here?"

"I've missed you, Em." His voice was soft. "I wanted to see you. May I come in?"

"Will, it's been over six months since I left Kansas, and I haven't heard a word from you. Why now?"

She stared at him as the crooked smile she knew so well played around his mouth. She couldn't leave him standing on her front porch. Emily sighed and stepped back.

"Come in," she said in a begrudging tone.

He walked through her door and back into her life after more than half a year's absence.

"I have a guest, the previous owner of this house."

She turned and walked toward the back of the house with Will following closely behind her.

"Garrett Loving," she said stiffly as they entered the kitchen, "Meet Will Forrester. He and I were friends when I lived in Kansas."

She watched as they sized each other up, each man looking the other up and down like boxers getting ready for their first round. Her anxiety deepened. One man was from her past, and one might possibly be in her future. This was too much anxiety to add to an already stressful day.

Garrett rose and reached to retrieve his hat. "I'll be going now, Emily. I'll give you a call in the morning to see when you want to start planting." He nodded his head at the other man. "Will."

Emily walked him to the door, where he leaned down and whispered into her ear, "Do I need to stay?"

She shook her head and assured him she would be fine.

"If you're sure," he said, "but please phone me if you need anything. I'm not certain I like his being here. I can get rid of him, if you want."

"Don't worry, Garrett, I'll be okay. I'll just find out why he's here and send him on his way. I'll see you about seven-thirty in the morning."

She forced her lips into a smile, hoping to set his mind at ease, and, at the same time, wanting the illusion to calm her own state of mind.

Emily hesitated at the door after closing it behind Garrett. Squaring her shoulders, she turned and walked back to the kitchen to face Will. While she was walking Garrett to the door, her ex had poured himself some coffee and sat at the table

———

74

drinking it.

"Okay, tell me the truth, Will. Why are you here? What do you want from me? You told me in very harsh words and a great deal of yelling to leave and never come back. I did. What's suddenly landed you on my doorstep?"

"You know I didn't mean all that stuff I said when I was upset." His face was set in the sardonic smile that was his one-size-fits-all ploy to get her to forgive him and let him back into her good graces.

"Come on, babe, we had some really good times together—you know we did. Don't tell me you can't remember how great it was for us at first. I missed you and wanted to see you. In fact, I came to take you home. I've got a good job now like you wanted me to have, and it'll be easy for you to find another one. You don't even have to work if you don't want to. Why, we can even get married, Em. That's what you wanted to do last year."

"I *am* home," Emily said. "I bought this house and plan to stay here. Miranda has a new baby boy, and I'm looking for a job. I am not leaving Texas."

Emily watched Will's face darken like an autumn sky, the fake smile obliterated by his quick temper, his lips curling into the familiar sneer.

"So, you're Miss Independence now?" He'd lost all pretence of control, and his voice rose stridently. "Who's the dude that was just here? You two have something going?"

"I told you, he's the previous owner of this house. He's also a friend who is helping me with my garden."

"Oh, I'll just bet he's *helping you*."

The innuendo was too much for Emily, and she exploded.

"Just who do you think you are, Will Forrester, coming in here and acting like you own me? We split up months ago. You do remember why we split, don't you? I told you I couldn't go on the way we were. You wanted me to support you so you could pursue your singing career, but you never really tried doing that, did you? Have you done anything whatsoever toward the career you were so sure about in the months I've been gone? Without me around to pay your bills?"

Folding her arms across her chest, Emily glared at him. "I've moved on with my life, just as I thought you'd done. There is nothing left for the two of us, so you may as well turn around and head back to Kansas. Alone."

His face dark red, Forrester scowled, and his eyes narrowed to slits. Emily didn't think he was capable of violence, but she'd never pushed him far enough to find out. She wished—too late—she'd taken Garrett up on his offer to stick around.

She winced as Will grabbed her arm in a tight grip.

"Let go of me!"

She wrenched her arm free and rubbed the purple marks she knew would become bruises.

He shook his head as if stubbornness would rule the day. "I've had enough of your foolishness, Em. It's time you came back home. Now, get your bags packed. We're going to Kansas."

"I'm not going anywhere with you, Will. You and I are through, and I never want to see you again. Now, please leave my house. Right now," she said with as much force as her five-foot-four frame could muster. The sound of her words conveyed more strength than she felt.

"Emily, I said for you to go get your bags," he insisted loudly as he grabbed her arm again. "You're coming with me where you belong. We can be home by midnight."

She tried without success to twist out of his grasp.

"Let go of me, Will. I'm not going anywhere with you, and I'm telling you one more time. Get out of my house." Her voice had risen above its normal volume as her own anger grew.

76

Suddenly, the back door flew open with a force that startled both of them, and Garrett Loving strode into the kitchen.

"Let go of her, Forrester, and walk out of this house before I'm forced to become unpleasant. The lady told you to go, and I think that's a good idea."

Garrett had a good three inches in height over Will and was more muscular, his biceps straining against his shirt sleeves. She watched several expressions flit over her ex-boyfriend's face as he considered his chances in a physical encounter with the man glowering at him. He dropped Emily's arm, but reached for her shoulders and forced her to face him.

"This isn't over, Emily. I'll be back."

Garrett walked over to stand beside her and gently took her arm. He looked at the bruise quickly forming and frowned.

"I don't think so, Forrester. I wouldn't advise it anyway if you know what's good for you. The door's that way."

He pointed. "Click your ruby red slippers and have a safe trip back to Kansas, Toto."

With a defiant glare at Emily's protector, Will turned on his heel and stalked toward the front door. A moment later it slammed, and Emily cringed as she worried about the door's vintage glass window.

"Thank you, Garrett. I'm sorry you had to witness that horrid scene, but I'm very glad you came back." She rubbed the discoloration on her arm. "Toto? I think Toto was the dog in the movie."

Garrett grinned. "Then, it's appropriate. I had a feeling he wasn't going to let you go so easily, so I waited out at the truck. When I heard raised voices, I felt you needed my help. I think you should come out to the ranch with me tonight, Emily, just so I'll know you're safe."

He waited while she put some clothing and her toothbrush

into a tote bag, and then took her arm and led her to his pickup in the driveway. It was a short drive out of town to his ranch, about ten miles north of town. They were both quiet on the way. Emily wondered what Garrett thought about the scene he'd witnessed.

She worried, knowing Will wasn't likely to leave town at Garrett's insistence or her own. He probably headed straight for a bar, and now had a beer bottle in his hand with his temper on the boil. If he hung around Cedar Valley, she knew he'd continue to harass her. Just when she'd felt her life was so together, she got hit with complications.

They arrived at the turn-off to Garrett's place as the sun was setting. Emily tugged her thoughts away from her current problems and directed her attention to what lay ahead: the ranch Garrett Loving mentioned often and obviously loved.

Chapter Eleven

The truck slowed and Garrett turned left off the highway— west, Emily reminded herself— onto a blacktop road marked by a sign that read, "Rose Lane." The lane was lined with massive oak trees, the limbs from each huge trunk reaching out toward its neighbors. They reminded Emily of the two mature trees that stood in front of Miss Rose's, . . . er, *her*, house. She wondered if whoever planted the trees meant for them to someday look as though they guarded the way to the ranch house.

They passed a one-story red brick house set close to the road just before the winding lane opened onto a large clearing and unveiled a magnificent log house. A faded red barn and a long stable building behind the house, plus cattle bunched together near a barbed-wire fence, made the place look like a real ranch— not quite what she'd been expecting. The deep reds, purples and grays of the sun setting behind the structure matched her somber mood.

Garrett took her hand as they walked up the circular drive. Two sturdy rocking chairs sat on either side of the knotty pine oversized door. It looked like a pleasant place to sit and enjoy the stars.

Garrett unlocked the door and held it open for her.

Her first impression of the interior was that of a rustic, but stylish, lodge. Two red leather sofas faced each other in the spacious living room. The fieldstone fireplace at one end of the room was so large Emily felt certain she could stand inside it without bending her head. In spite of its size, the room looked cozy and welcoming. She imagined a fire roaring in the grate and smiling people, Garrett among them, enjoying themselves in this room.

She smiled. "This is very nice."

"Thanks. The ranch has been in the family for over one hundred years. There's a guest room two doors down this hall on the right. It's comfortable and quiet, with all the amenities, as they say."

"Do you often have guests stay here?" Emily asked.

"No, at least not overnight. When friends or business colleagues come out from Dallas, they usually stay at a hotel. Not many city types want to bunk in a ranch house built of logs. Oh, they'll come out here for a few hours wearing cowboy hats and boots and pretend they're roughing it, but then they want to go someplace they can't hear crickets chirping at dusk.

"My city friends like night life, and not the kind you find out here at the ranch—not sitting on the porch in a rocker looking at the stars up above in that big beautiful Texas sky. But I do occasionally conduct business meetings here. It's a comfortable home away from home and has just the right touch of casualness when I need a less formal atmosphere than the board room in Dallas. The ranch atmosphere—especially the livestock—made a big impression on some visiting Japanese investors.

"Forgive my lack of manners. Would you like something to eat or drink? The fridge is kept well stocked. My foreman lives on the property, looks after the ranch, makes sure there's always plenty of food on hand, and really takes good care of the place. He started work here when he was a young man. He and my dad were great friends. I'm usually here on weekends, holidays, and for at least a month during the summer. "

"Oh, is this a working ranch? I assumed it was just your weekend retreat."

"Of course, it's a working ranch. I raise Longhorn cattle and several types of hay. When I'm here, I spend my time building fences, buying and selling cattle, actually getting my hands dirty. I'm not one of those big-city guys who sit at a desk during the week and head for the country to play cowboy on weekends."

Did she detect a note of defensiveness in his tone?

"I didn't mean to imply you don't really work here, Garrett. I don't know much about working ranches, and since you have businesses in the city, I just thought . . ."

The door flew open with such force it banged against the wall and bounced away from it. Will stood in the doorway, the depth of his fury etched on his face so deeply that Emily shrank back a step. His eyes glittered with hatred, his jaws were tightly set, and his fists were clinched. He looked dangerous.

Sudden fear gripped her, and she glanced at Garrett. He stepped between her and the furious man, taking two more long steps past the bar and into the living room. One hand behind him, he motioned for Emily to stay where she was.

"You're trespassing on private property, Forrester. You'd better leave right now before I throw you out."

As he spoke, Garrett reached for a small remote and pressed a button.

"You won't get rid of me so fast," the intruder snarled. "I'm taking Emmy with me this time, and don't try to stop me. She belongs with me in Kansas."

He moved toward Emily, and Garrett stepped in front of her. Will's fist connected with her protector's jaw.

Crack!

Emily backed further away as the two men struggled, locked in combat and trading blows. A lamp crashed to the floor, shards of broken glass scattering. In rising panic, she grabbed her cell phone from her pocket and dialed 911.

"Help! We need help—quickly!" she yelled into the phone over the sound of the battle raging across the room and told the dispatcher to send officers from the sheriff's office to the Loving ranch. Fortunately, she wasn't asked for an address, since everyone here seemed to know Garrett. Fear had rendered her mind blank regarding the highway number, distance from town, even the name of the lane to the ranch.

"Hurry!" she gasped, so alarmed she was afraid she might pass out. Slipping the phone back into her pocket, she consciously slowed her breathing. She could be of no help to Garrett if she hyperventilated and passed out.

The sounds of the fight punctuated her frantic thoughts as she looked around the room for something she could use as a weapon. There were fireplace tools on the hearth, but they were sharp and might be capable of lethal damage. Will could wrest something like that away from her and use it on Garrett. The horror of that thought made Emily cringe, forcing her to acknowledge her true feelings. She couldn't bear the thought of Garrett being injured, or worse . . .

Move! Find something to help Garrett!

Her emotions churned as she sought something sturdy that wasn't lethally sharp, but before she could grab one of the pans hanging from the kitchen rack, four men burst through the doorway. Two wore uniforms and a third held a shotgun, which he pointed at Will. The last man wore faded denim jeans and jacket, topped by a worn cowboy hat, and he stood motionless off to one side as though his role was only that of spectator, an extra.

One of the uniformed men grabbed Will, pulled him away from Garrett and held him as the other handcuffed his wrists and patted him down, retrieving a small handgun tucked inside one of his boots.

"Will Forrester, you're under arrest for breaking and entering, conspiracy to kidnap, assault and battery, and carrying a concealed weapon." The officer launched into the spiel of the

Miranda warning.

The man who held the shotgun, which was now passed along to one of the uniformed men, appeared to be in charge. He asked, "You okay, Mr. Loving?"

"I'm fine, Eric. Thanks for getting here so quickly. This is Emily Parker. Emily—Eric Bolton, our county sheriff."

Bolton pulled a small notebook from his pocket, flipped it open and jotted something on one of its pages. He flipped it closed and returned it to his pocket.

"The Kansas PD called and alerted city police this guy might be in the area. Seems he did a lot of bragging in a bar out there about how he was heading to Cedar Valley, Texas, planning to drag his girlfriend, Emily Parker, back to Kansas no matter what it took, hinting he wasn't above "putting some hurt on her and tying her up if necessary," . . . er, you, that is, ma'am. The bartender notified police and they called Cedar Valley PD. They found your address, and a neighbor said he saw you leave with Mr. Loving after an unknown man stormed off, got it in a dented pickup and drove away. These guys called me on the radio, and we were on our way to the ranch when we heard from the dispatcher.

"Forrester's wanted in Abilene for several felony offenses. Now we'll add new charges. He looks to be out of commission for a while, by my reckoning."

Emily trembled, and Garrett hugged her gently.

"He came to my house earlier tonight and demanded I go with him," she told the sheriff. "I refused, and Garrett asked him to leave. He gave in and left, which surprised me, but said he'd be back. I was afraid he wouldn't give up so easily, but didn't expect him to come to the ranch."

"I thought she'd be safer out here tonight," Garrett told the sheriff. "He must have followed us."

"I don't think he'll bother you any more, Ms. Parker. We'll

keep him in custody until he's extradited for those felony charges waiting in Kansas. He's facing an indictment. After they get through with him, I suspect the charges here will extend his sentence. He'll likely do time in Kansas and then be transferred to one of our four-star Texas hotels with razor wire decor. It should be quite a while before he gets out."

She watched as her former boyfriend was led out the front door in handcuffs, the scowl on his face overlaid by bruises and a bleeding cut over one eye from the fight. She wondered what happened during the months she'd been in Texas that made him go off the deep end. Had he been in trouble with the law before she met him and kept it hidden from her? What had he done in Kansas that warranted felony charges? She thought of the gun Garrett hadn't given him time to draw and shivered. Thank goodness she hadn't stayed with Will. How lucky she was to have met a reliable and protective man like Garrett Loving.

Turning, she saw him in deep conversation with the man who had accompanied the policeman and sheriff. There was a darkening bruise on Garrett's right cheek and a scrape on his chin, but otherwise he seemed none the worse for the fight. He was obviously in fit shape with good self-defense skills.

He noticed her gaze and closed the gap between them, placing a protective arm around Emily's shoulders and drawing her close to his side.

"Emily, this is Hank Reynolds, my most trusted friend and foreman. He takes care of the ranch while I'm gone. That's his house that sits at the front of the property near the gates. Hank, this is Emily Parker."

"Hello, Ms Parker. Glad to meet you."

He tipped his hat above his thinning hair in the same manner Garrett used. Emily thought it must be a particularly Western gesture. How had she missed noticing it all these years? Probably because there was a distinct lack of gentlemen in her life after Chris died, and he'd never worn a hat.

"I'm almost always here if you need anything, ma'am. I'll be going now, Garrett, unless you need me for something else. Day starts early tomorrow."

"Don't they all? You go ahead, Hank. I think we're fine here. Thanks for coming so fast."

Garrett shook Reynolds' hand and walked him to the door. Then he closed it and fastened the deadbolt.

"Are you okay, Emily?"

"I am now. How about you, Garrett? You have a bruise on your cheek and a painful-looking scrape on your chin. I'm so sorry you had to get involved in this, especially having to fight with Will. Are you hurt anywhere else?"

At the shake of his head, she quickly exhaled, "I don't know what happened to him after I left. I've never seen him act so brutal, sink to physical violence instead of just talking mean. I'm glad your foreman was nearby. "

Garrett held up the remote.

"This alarm sounds in Hank's house and is only used in emergencies. I had it installed a few months ago, and I'm sure glad I did. Come sit down, Emily. You're still shaking. I'll make us some coffee."

He guided her to one of the sofas, kissed her softly on the forehead, and walked around the bar into the kitchen. She heard the comforting sounds of a kitchen in use, cabinet doors opening and closing, water running.

Emily's heart still pounded, and adrenaline flooded her body. She rehearsed the scenes of the past hour. She couldn't bear to think of what might have happened if Will had managed to get hold of that gun.

It was all surreal. Thank goodness Garrett was there to

protect her.

"Sure you're okay?" he asked as he handed her a steaming coffee mug, and she breathed in its rich aroma. "You seemed to be in another world just then, or perhaps I should say, another state. I'm sure that brawl and the news about Forrester's trouble with the law upset you. Are you still in love with the guy?" he asked.

Worry darted across his face with the question.

"Oh, no, Garrett—quite the contrary. I'm just trying to figure out why he wanted me to go back to Kansas. The only thing I can assume is that he needed something and wanted me to provide it. He used me before, for transportation, fuel, food, hotels, clothes and anything else he needed that cost money he wouldn't work to earn. He looks like a grownup, but has a kid's mentality and an oversized sense of entitlement."

With the startling news of his felony charges in Kansas, she thought her resources may have represented a chance for him to escape the law. Now he had even more charges to face, and she was relieved he was locked up in jail.

"When I first met Will, he told me that he was working hard to make it big as a singer in Nashville, but his bad attitude turned off booking agents and club managers. He couldn't understand why other singers got the engagements he thought should be his. Besides that, he didn't have the talent to become a star, only he wouldn't face that fact."

She remembered him shouting, "No one understands me!" on the night he stormed out of her apartment and, she thought, out of her life until he resurfaced today.

"I supported him at first. Helped him with his bookings and paid for demo recordings. We always used my car and gas, and I paid the hotel bills and for meals until I realized he only wanted me for what I could do for him. He didn't care about me. He

86

simply wanted everything handed to him on a platter. There would be no paying of dues for Will Forrester."

"Our final fight that led to the break happened after he heard of some big opportunity—he said—available in Nashville, and he wanted my car and some cash to make the trip. When I refused, he threw a fit and stormed out. I phoned Miranda and told her about the situation I could put up with no longer. She told me to leave, to just get in my car and drive away, that I was welcome to stay with them.

"I knew she was right, so I found an all-night trailer rental place in the phone book, had a trailer hitch installed on my SUV at a truck stop and drove away pulling my worldly goods at two in the morning. I never heard a word from Will that night or after I arrived in Cedar Valley. I thought the whole ordeal was over and done."

Garrett enfolded her in the circle of his arms. She snuggled into his embrace, and all seemed right with her world in spite of Will and the upheavals he'd caused. At least they didn't have to worry about him coming back, because he was in jail and would return to face a judge in Kansas.

Garrett pulled her closer and she heard him whisper against her hair, "I could get used to having you by my side, here at the ranch."

But after a few peaceful moments in his arms, before she drifted off to sleep, another thought took the place of Will Forrester. The ghost of *Miss Rose* dominated Emily's mind as she snuggled further into the arms of that woman's only son.

Chapter Twelve

Emily pulled the baby-soft blanket over her shoulders and wriggled her nose at the aromas of fresh coffee and cooked bacon. Even before opening her eyes, she could feel a presence on the side of her bed.

Wait, this isn't my bed.

She was now fully awake and almost knocked the coffee cup from Garrett's hand as she bolted up . . . in his bed.

"Wh—what am I doing in your bed? We didn't . . . you didn't. . .?"

Garrett smiled sheepishly. "You aren't in my bed, Emily. You're in the guest bedroom at my ranch. I carried you in here last night after you fell asleep on the sofa. Don't worry. I didn't remove anything but your shoes."

Emily sighed with relief. Now that she was wide awake, she realized Garrett would never take advantage of her or any woman's vulnerability. His courtly behavior might seem a bit old-fashioned, like something out of a classic Western, but he was a true gentleman.

She realized that she probably had Miss Rose to thank for that. Garrett called his mother old-fashioned, and she was the person who had great influence over him as a youth. No doubt she set out to make her son a man who would behave in most situations with courtesy and consideration. That is, unless he had to defend a woman from a bully with his fists.

Memories of the brawl Will started the previous night flooded her mind and she closed her eyes again. As she lay back on the pillows, she said, "Oh, Garrett, what must you think about what happened with Will? I'm so very sorry." Emily covered her face with both hands. When she looked at him again, she asked, "Are you certain you're okay? Nothing's broken?"

"I'm fine. It would take a lot more than Forrester to put me out of commission. You don't need to apologize for him, Emily. His behavior is his own responsibility, not yours, and some of the things he's done will land him in prison. Be thankful you left him when you did. I spoke with Eric this morning, and the Kansas Troopers are on their way to get him and take him back to face a Kansas judge and jury.

"So don't bother your pretty little head about him. Concentrate on what we're going to plant in our garden. I have breakfast ready, and as soon as you want, we'll head for your house."

Standing at the bathroom sink, looking in the mirror as she brushed her hair, she wondered what Garrett meant when he said he could get used to her by his side at the ranch. He'd told her earlier he intended to pursue her, but hadn't he pursued a lot of women? What about all those women he was photographed with in Dallas? Had he said the same sweet things to them in the thrill of the chase? Wasn't that how playboys operated? Turn on the charm for every woman as though she's the only one?

When she'd feared for his safety the night before, she understood how much she cared for the man, but in the harsh light of day, that realization only frightened her. Could she really trust her judgment about any man after falling for someone like Will Forrester? Now she felt herself falling for Garrett Loving.

If the rumors about all of Garrett's women were true, would she be only another conquest for him, another trophy for his hat rack? Was he the love-'em- and-leave-'em type who needed the adoration of many women and could not be happy for long with only one?

Emily looked at her reflection in the mirror and gave herself a silent pep talk. After escaping the likes of Will Forrester, she shouldn't be thinking so soon about another relationship, especially one with a man desired by so many women and who probably wanted them too—for a time, at least. How could she feel secure in such a match? Wouldn't she just be waiting for him to get tired of her when another face attracted him?

Why get free of one hopeless liaison only to jump straight into another based strictly on emotions rather than using her brain?

Girl—get a grip on your feelings! You're responsible for your own happiness and peace of mind. It's time you proved you're a strong woman, not a doormat for a pair of cowboy boots.

By the time she walked into the kitchen, Emily's mood had gone through a sea change. Her mind was firmly in control of her emotions, and she was determined that her actions would follow suit.

Garrett stood at the kitchen bar, coffee pot in hand, and poured a mug of coffee that he handed to Emily. "Sit anywhere you like. I've got bacon, scrambled eggs and pancakes for breakfast. I thought we could use a hearty breakfast before the real work in the garden begins."

"Thanks, Garrett, and I'm sorry you went to all that trouble, but I'm not hungry this morning. Besides, I think you've already done more than enough for me. Thank you for tilling the garden and all of your many generosities since I moved here, especially your gallant defense of me yesterday. I'm still embarrassed that you had to protect me from that ruffian Will with your fists. But enough is enough. I don't expect you to give up all your time to look after me, and I'm sure you have work here to do on your ranch. If you don't mind giving me a ride back to my house, you can get back to your ranching chores."

Emily's heart ached at the pain she saw in Garrett's eyes. Her coffee cup clattered and sloshed coffee as she set it on the bar, but she hurried for the door, grabbing her jacket on the way.

"But Emily, I don't understand."

Garrett caught her arm and turned her to face him before she could unlock the deadbolt and open the front door.

"What did I do? Are you upset because I punched Will? I asked you last night if you were still in love with him, and I believe your answer was no. Wasn't that true? Are you still in love with him after all?"

"No, I'm not in love with him, Garrett. If I ever was, he definitely cured me of that insanity. I simply think it would be better if you and I didn't see each other for a while. Surely you realize that after ending the disastrous relationship I had with Will, my focus now should be on getting a job and spending time with my family. It's too soon to think of . . . having feelings . . . for someone else. Yes, it's much too soon."

The look on Garrett's face made Emily feel as though every word she uttered was a dagger stabbing his heart, so she looked away from him to stay strong. She'd made a promise to her reflection in the mirror, and she must not give in to feelings—her own or anyone else's. It was time to let her brain rather than her heart make the decisions that affected her life.

Without another word, Garrett took his coat and hat from the stand beside the door. Silently, he put them on and opened the door for Emily. She walked across the threshold and onto the porch, hurried down the steps and out to the truck. She heard his boots walking slowly behind her.

On the drive back to her house, he asked, "Is it my mother? Do you really believe she doesn't want us to be together?"

"Too much has happened since we began seeing each other, Garrett. I don't know what to think about any of it. I've been awakened nearly every night in my house with doors slamming and clumping noises like boots tromping through the house—noises that can't be explained. Is your mother causing them? I don't know, but the fact that they happen every time I'm with you or talk to you on the phone seems to suggest it is. I know you think I'm imagining these things, but I swear to you I'm not.

"Then yesterday, that horrid commotion with Will barging in and starting a fight—*he* was horrid, not you—but the entire situation was nerve-wracking for me and a reminder that I got involved with a man who turned out to be totally opposite from the person I thought he was, which is solid proof I didn't get to know that man well enough before trusting him. I took him at face value and allowed my emotions to control my decisions rather than my brain. That reminder is more than enough to scare me.

"Who knows? Maybe something or someone is trying to tell us we shouldn't be together. Whatever or whoever it is, we need to cool things for a while. I need to be alone to think about what I want in life with no distractions to cloud my judgment. I hope you will try to understand that, Garrett, and that you'll honor my wishes."

They arrived at Emily's house. Before he opened his truck door and walked around to open hers, he said, "Emily, you're making a mistake. We make a good team, and I want you in my life. I know I could make you happy. I just want a chance."

She got out of the truck and hurried to the front door, almost running, key in her outstretched hand. She unlocked and opened it the door quickly, closing it behind her as soon as she was inside. She knew without looking that Garrett had followed her and stood alone on her front porch wondering why she shut the door in his face. She couldn't bear to look at the hurt in his sky-blue eyes, knowing she was the cause.

She leaned back against the wall beside the door, tears

streaming from her eyes, until she heard the sound of his boots moving away from the door and down the steps. In a few moments, she heard the sound of his truck engine, which grew fainter as he drove away. She slid down the wall to the floor, pulled her knees up under her chin, and cried as though her heart was breaking.

Well, Emily, my girl, she told herself later as she wiped her eyes, *you did it. You kept your promise to yourself and drove him away. I hope that's what you want, because he's gone. If you change your mind, it may be too late.*

Chapter Thirteen

Feeling the dampness of the soil against her hands and using rusty muscles was cathartic to some extent for Emily during the next few days. She planted spring flowers beside the walkway and in the flower beds after she finished putting in her garden. Then she painted two small tables a shade of bright blue to go beside the wicker chairs on the back porch. She stayed busy with everything she could think of to do, trying to distract her thoughts from Garrett Loving.

Yet, even when she was working, his words rolled through her mind like that battery-operated bunny in the commercial, going and going without any letup. She kept visualizing the hurt on his face after she made her speech proclaiming the need to be alone. Yes, Garrett seemed to be such a nice man, but hadn't she thought Will was nice when they were first together? Could the motives of any man really be trusted when he was trying to make a woman care for him? Wouldn't he be on his best behavior? But, the problem was, would that behavior last? Would the loving words continue? Loving. Just the sound of his name started the tears again.

Even though she'd been happily married for many years and never doubted her husband's love or fidelity, Emily's unhappy experience with Will now made her distrust her own judgment when it came to love. She might choose the wrong man again and not know it until she faced heartbreak. How could she take such a chance? Wasn't being alone better than being with the wrong man?

Emily felt she would be all right as soon as she could control her thoughts and marshal the inner strength she knew she possessed, but the gap in her life that Garrett left when he drove away seemed huge just now. He was the first thought on her mind when she awoke and the last before she went to sleep each night, and all the time in-between, no matter how much busywork she found to do.

She focused on chores that needed to be done in and around her home, and she intensified her job search, branching out to all the larger suburbs. Her money wouldn't last forever, and she couldn't exactly ask Garrett for job contacts now that she'd practically thrown him out of her life.

As she put away the last of the folded laundry one morning, Emily heard the creak of the back door and Miranda calling out, "Mom, we've come to pay a visit."

"Hello, little Chris," Emily said as Miranda handed the baby to her for a cuddle. Cradling him in her arms she asked, "How's my little man today?"

"He's fine, but the question is—how are you, Mom? We haven't seen you in nearly two weeks, since the day after that awful Will tried to attack you. You haven't heard from him again, have you?

"No, I haven't heard from him and hope I don't. He was extradited to Kansas for felonies he committed there—what, I don't know and don't care to learn. I'm just glad he's gone, and I never want to see him again."

Miranda studied her mother's face. "What about Garrett? Have you seen him?"

"Not since the next morning after Will made his appearance, when he drove me home."

"Why not?"

This whole thing with Will jolted me back to reality, Miranda, that's why. It's better if I don't get involved with anyone for a while. Besides, if I'm not mistaken, it was you who warned me about all of Garrett's women, and I don't want to be just one of many."

Miranda smiled as she handed her mother a burp pad for the baby.

"Mom, Garrett came to see me a few days ago."

Emily wasn't sure she wanted to hear what followed, but knowing her daughter, she would hear it anyway. She patted her grandson on his back and was rewarded with an audible burp.

"He said you told him it would be better not to continue the relationship. Mom, I didn't even know you two were in a relationship. I don't think you've confided very much in me lately, or maybe I've been too busy with the baby and finishing my book to realize you and Garrett were getting serious.

"At any rate, he looked very unhappy and said he wants to talk to you but is afraid to jeopardize any progress he's made so far. He told me how you feel about his mother and the door slamming, which you already told me. He said you think Miss Rose doesn't want the two of you to be together. Is that true? Are you going to let a cranky old lady's spirit keep you from finding true romance and happiness?"

Emily rocked the baby in her arms and gathered her thoughts before she spoke. Finally, she looked at her daughter and spoke from her heart.

"Mandy, I care for Garrett, a lot. In fact, I'm pretty sure I'm falling in love with him. But I made such a mistake when I trusted Will. Looking back at how badly our relationship deteriorated in a short time made me think about what I want out of life . . . and what I don't want.

"Will was never physically abusive to me in Kansas, but he was verbally abusive, and I put up with it. Garrett is too kind to treat me or anyone that way, but I'm still afraid to get involved with him this quickly. I told him it would be better if we didn't see

---

each other for a while. I need to think it through, Mandy."

Mandy looked at her mother and sighed. "Well, Mom, it's your life, and you can do whatever you like. I just want you to know that the man who sat in my kitchen is hurting badly, and it's my opinion that you should see him or at least talk to him on the phone with more of an explanation. He's done a lot for you. Don't you think you at least owe him enough of a conversation that he doesn't blame himself for losing you? He thinks he did something to change your mind about him."

Emily watched Miranda walk out the door, baby Chris strapped close to her body in his soft quilted carrier. She thought about her daughter's suggestion and knew she wanted to see Garrett as badly as he wanted to see her. Miranda's confidence to her about Garrett's visit and how he'd poured out his feelings so freely touched Emily and made her wonder if her own behavior to him was fair. After all, his reputation as a lady's man could be solely derived from photographs in the newspapers and rumors garnered from those pictures. Was it right of her to judge him on the basis of gossip without giving him an opportunity to defend himself?

The battle in her mind surged on. Should she see him, or shouldn't she? Emily was torn, but knew she'd have to decide soon. She was no nearer peace of mind than she'd been two weeks ago, and all the chores in the world couldn't keep Garrett Loving out of her thoughts or stop her from wanting to feel his lips on hers again.

Am I being a strong woman, or am I just punishing myself for making the wrong choice with Will? And, if I'm punishing myself, am I also punishing Garrett for something he didn't do?

It was a conundrum, and only she could solve it.

Chapter Fourteen

Emily sat on her sofa after Miranda and the baby left, her legs pulled up on its cushions and a soft throw pillow clutched against her chest. Fourteen long, lonely days ago she'd left Garrett's ranch with the intent to stop seeing him so she wouldn't fall more deeply in love with him. It was an attempt to prevent more heartache, but it hadn't worked. From the moment she closed her front door against Garrett, she'd felt loneliness and depression, and those feelings intensified every day.

She'd expected the gardening and painting into which she threw her energies to calm her feelings, but every plant that went into the moist ground reminded her of the day Garrett tilled the soil. As she worked, she visualized his arm muscles flexing as he pushed the tiller and heard him whistle cheerfully while he worked. She closed her eyes and saw him lean back and place his hands on his back after he finished the chore.

No, work didn't soothe her emotions one bit. Her feelings for Garrett only deepened. Running away from him hadn't saved her from losing her heart. Now she admitted to herself how much she loved him.

I love you, Garrett, with all of my heart. I hope you still want me.

* * *

"Garrett, this is Emily."

She spoke into the phone, trying to keep her voice steady while her heart beat a staccato rhythm. For three days after Mandy's visit—three days that moved with a snail's pace—Emily contemplated a call to Garrett and worried about his possible reaction. Would he speak to her or hang up in disgust? For three days, these thoughts left her too drained and shaky to follow through with the call.

On the fourth day, she mustered up the courage to key in his phone number and inhaled deeply as she listened to the ringer. Once . . . twice . . . and then she heard his deep voice, that strong yet gentle voice that sent shivers throughout her body.

"I'm so glad you called, Emily. I've wanted to call you, but was unsure if you'd talk to me or hang up the phone."

She laughed with relief, engulfed by a sudden weakness as her tense muscles relaxed. Her hand holding the phone felt as though it changed from flesh, sinew and bone to melting fondue. She sank into the nearest chair and leaned her head back against the upholstery.

"I've thought the same thing, Garrett, for the past three days."

"Can we meet and talk this thing out, Emily? I want to look into your beautiful eyes when you try to convince me that we shouldn't see each other. I've missed you . . . a lot. Is it all right if I come over now?"

"If it's all the same to you, Garrett, let's not meet here. I'd rather see you at the ranch. I can leave now. I'm afraid if I wait, I'll chicken out." After a slight pause, she whispered, "I've missed you too . . . a lot."

As she drove, Emily wondered how to explain her abrupt action to Garrett. He knew some aspects of her calamitous relationship with Will, but she must make him aware how much that experience scarred her emotionally and made her afraid to risk commitment. The way Will took advantage of her while she was with him exacted a harsh toll on Emily's psyche. She was afraid to let herself trust again.

She thought of her final night in Kansas when they'd

quarreled bitterly. Among the many horrible things he shouted at her was his drunken threat that he'd make sure no one else wanted her after he finished with her. Now that she'd seen how violent he could become, she was thankful she'd left that night. She might have become a crime victim statistic if she'd stayed.

By the time she arrived back in Texas, Emily had gone over every word and action of that quarrel until she knew it by heart, asking herself if she'd overreacted or if she'd dodged a bullet. It didn't take her long to realize she hadn't overreacted—she hadn't acted soon enough, before Will nearly wrecked her self-esteem.

Would she ever stop beating herself up emotionally over the mistake of judgment she made with Will Forrester? Wasn't everyone entitled to at least one wrong decision of the heart? Hadn't she learned from that experience—enough to make the right choice if given another chance?

* * *

Garrett was restless as he waited for Emily, waiting to discover if she would agree to be part of his life, or if the misery Forrester put her through made her too gun shy to take a chance on love. He sat on the cool leather sofa for a few minutes, but tension made him jump up and pace the floor. Up and down, up and down the room he walked as he thought of her words on the phone. They hadn't told him much, but her voice sounded hopeful, and the fact that she wanted to talk made him cautiously optimistic.

Garrett understood her hesitation and fears. It was his job to reassure her that he'd never treat her badly, never give her cause to regret being with him, but would always cherish her.

He had to make her believe that, because it was true. He'd found the woman of his dreams, the woman he wanted to share every part of his life with, for the rest of his life, and he couldn't bear the thought of losing her. He'd waited long enough to find his soul mate, and now he must convince Emily that he was the right man for her.

Although most people in Cedar Valley probably thought his boyhood was idyllic, growing up with a doting mother who gave him everything he could want, in actuality it was less than perfect. He'd loved Miss Rose and witnessed her many kindnesses to other people, a trait he felt he'd inherited from her, so he admired her goodness.

Kindness came natural to Garrett, and he never thought himself better than anyone else because he'd been born into affluence, inherited even more wealth, and become successful in business. At heart, he was a simple man who had decent values and integrity, and he could be relied upon—a man who embodied the phrase, *what you see is what you get*.

While Miss Rose saw to it that Garrett was at want for nothing material and even anticipated what he might want—providing it before it could even become a wish—his mother also nearly suffocated him with her overbearing love. Her growing insistence that she would choose the *right* girl for him made his adolescent years not only difficult, but almost unbearable during that time when peer acceptance is so important. She scrutinized every girl he brought home, and no one met her standards.

It wasn't long before he stopped taking anyone home to meet her, and not long after that he stopped dating altogether because he didn't want to lose his heart to a Cedar Valley girl who would be met by his mother with disdain. The only way he could maintain his good relationship with his widowed mother, which was important to him, was to ensure he wasn't forced into a choice between a special girl and Miss Rose.

Word got around town that his mother had a tight rein on him, and no girl who hadn't already experienced it wanted to be subjected to Miss Rose's intimidation. The younger children in town loved her, but teenage girls feared her.

Garrett continued to respect his mother for raising him alone after his father's death, but he often wondered how different his life might have been had his father lived.

After college and his entry into the business world, it seemed appropriate to have a beautiful girl on his arm at parties for photo ops. There was a procession of pretty girls, many of them pageant winners from small Texas towns who moved to Dallas in search of a wealthy husband. He rarely had a third date with any of them because, by then, it was evident he wasn't looking for a wife, and they were all looking for well-to-do first husbands.

It was a joke among the young men with whom he worked in those early years in Dallas that the prettiest girls viewed the city, as well as Ft. Worth, as a hunting ground for a rich husband. Most were perfectly satisfied to become a trophy wife for older wealthy men who would either die while they were still young and attractive enough to marry for love or, once they got past the inevitable ten-year clause of the pre-nuptial agreement, obtain a divorce with a financial settlement that established them for life and allowed them to live it on their own terms.

Garrett never looked down on them for their motives. He enjoyed their company for a date or two, but their faces and names became blurred in his memory, and he never bothered to learn anything personal about any of them. As he grew older, the pretty women he escorted to splashy events were a bit older, used a bit more makeup, and added more highlights to their hair, but there was never any romantic spark between him and any of them. They were still looking for a rich husband, but he wasn't looking for a predatory wife.

The few women he actually dated with pleasure over the years tended toward ordinary looks, intelligence, talent, and non-dramatic behavior. But there were still no fireworks. These women were more like good friends than romantic interests. He'd decided that marriage and a family were not in the cards for him when he met Emily Parker. At this stage of his life, family would be a package deal consisting of an adult married daughter, son-in-law and grandchild (possibly other grandkids), but he truly felt for the first time in his life that he was in love.

He knew right away when he met Emily that she was different from all the other women he'd encountered. She was real—beautiful and serene, yes—but still a down-to-earth woman who didn't pretend to be something she wasn't. She was smart and talented, caring and kindhearted. Emily fit into the same mold as Garrett. *What you see is what you get.*

What Garrett wanted where Emily was concerned was to get to know her well, to learn everything she liked and disliked, what made her laugh and what made those lovely blue eyes sparkle, those things in life that were truly important to her. He felt he'd already made some progress there, but believed he could spend the rest of his life learning new things about this woman. She was the first woman he'd met who made him feel with certainty he wanted to grow old with her, but how could he convince her of his sincerity? How could he get past that wall her fear had built between them? Whatever it took, he knew he had to try. It was the most important thing in his life now.

Chapter Fifteen

Turning into the secluded lane that led to the ranch house, Emily breathed deeply to help her relax. She could do this. She could open up to Garrett about her life, about Will, her fear of commitment, and, yes, Miss Rose.

Miss Rose.

Will she ever accept her son being with me? Do I measure up to her standards?

This was the big question plaguing her. She felt she could overcome the apprehension caused by Will's treatment of her, but she believed Miss Rose would always remain nearby watching over her son and possibly coming between Emily and Garrett. She watched as Garrett walked from the porch to her car. He opened the door, took her hand and gently helped her from the car and enfolded her in his arms. She smiled at him and looked into his eyes as her own arms encircled his waist. This felt so good, so right, and so safe.

Then his lips found hers, and there was no pretense in that kiss, no holding back the love they both felt for each other.

At last he released her and stepped back to look in her face, his fears relieved as though he could read her mind. Perhaps he could, for she'd held nothing back in the kiss that warmed his very soul.

"I'm very glad you called, Emily. I'll tell you a little secret. If I hadn't heard from you today, I would have only waited a few more hours, and then I would have called you. I couldn't wait any longer. Come on inside and let's talk."

He put his arm around her shoulders and escorted her up the

walk, across the porch and into the great room. He sat on one end of a large sofa and drew her gently down beside him, holding her closely. He'd missed her closeness after she left, more than he'd thought possible.

As for Emily, she reveled in the sensuous feel of the soft leather, the strong gentleness of Garrett's arms, and the feeling that she was cherished.

"It feels wonderful, Garrett . . . being here, I mean. I love this place, and I love being with you."

As they gazed into each other's eyes, she summoned her courage to confess how she felt.

"I've been very lonely, and I've missed you every day. I think you realize how I feel about you, but I need to explain why I didn't think we should be together. I'm sure I seemed to be sending you mixed messages."

Garrett grinned and kissed the top of her head.

"I like the part where you said, you *didn't* think we should be together. Does the past tense mean you changed your mind?"

"I think . . . no, I'm sure I'm falling in love with you, Garrett, but I was terribly afraid of my feelings after the failed relationship with Will. I was so hurt and disillusioned when I came back to Texas—a feeling I never wanted to experience again. I thought I'd rather be alone than live with the fear of being hurt and mistreated, wondering when the other shoe would drop, feeling inadequate and putting up with fights and accusations.

"I already told you Will was verbally abusive to me. Oh, it didn't start out that way. In the beginning, we had fun together. He was sweet to me and treated me well. But everything changed when he had trouble getting bookings. He refused to believe it could be his fault, that he wasn't talented enough for the big time. There was a huge change in his behavior, and I became his scapegoat. He took all of his frustrations out on me. It's terrible to become someone's emotional punching bag."

"Emily, just let it go, my dear. He'll never hurt you again. I'll see to that, and as for me, I promise I'll never hurt you, ever. I'll sign a declaration to that effect and post it in the town hall for everyone to see if you like." He pulled her closer to him. "Now, let's talk about us, about our being together, I mean. I love you, Emily, and I want you in my life. Permanently."

"Garrett, in spite of our feelings for each other, I still think we need to proceed slowly for a while. We should get to know each other thoroughly, our interests and values, all the things that people should know about each other before they make a commitment.

She paused and wrinkled her forehead in thought.

"Then, of course, there's Miss Rose. I know you think I'm imagining her, Garrett, but I promise you—she's in my house and makes her presence known every time you're there with me. I don't think she wants us to be together."

Emily sighed and snuggled closer to Garrett.

"My mother is gone, and has been for many years," he said. "True, the house remained empty after she was gone until you moved in, but I had someone clean it weekly, and neither they nor I ever heard anything like you've described.

"Don't get that look on your face, darlin'—I'm not saying you're wrong, just that she never made her presence known to me or anyone else but you."

Garrett wasn't sure how to convince Emily that his mother was gone and wouldn't be coming back. How could he be sure of that himself when he didn't understand how her presence might still be in the house so long after her death? He was open-minded enough to realize there are mysteries in the world that humans may not understand. He only knew that Emily believed his mother was a spirit in the house she'd bought from him, and that was enough for Garrett.

Of all people, he more than anyone knew the strength of will his mother had during her lifetime. She'd intimidated any girl he was attracted to when he was young in her determination to choose for him. If it was possible after death to somehow part the veil back into this world . . . Well, he didn't want Miss Rose to intimidate Emily. He wanted the woman he loved to feel safe, secure and unafraid, and he'd do whatever it took to achieve that end.

"Why don't we have dinner and discuss landscaping ideas I have for your house? There are tools in the storage building out back, and we can rummage through them and see what we have to work with. We'll have dinner in town and then come back and browse through some of the stuff Mom left behind that I stored out here. I've meant for a while to clean it out, but just didn't have the time, and it didn't seem pressing. Now it seems more important.

"There are some boxes in the storage building that Mom had packed away in her attic. They've been stored here since soon after her death, and it might be fun to find out together what they contain. I don't think she ever threw anything away."

Dinner in the small town consisted of a sandwich at the local Lazy Heart Grill. It was a simple meal, but delicious. Emily's appetite had been minimal since the day she left Garrett's ranch determined to break up with him, but now she was ravenous. He seemed more at ease than he had when she arrived at his place earlier that day, and he ate with obvious enjoyment.

"Emily, I'm serious regarding your concerns about my mother. Even if you do suspect her presence is lingering in your house, why wouldn't she want us to be together?"

"I don't know, Garrett, unless she feels betrayed that you want me in your life permanently without her permission. I didn't know her, so I can only guess, but I have the feeling you became her obsession after your father died. Maybe she wants you to pine for her the rest of your life.

"I know that sounds crazy. That's what I'd think if it happened to someone else and I only heard the story, but I know it's real because I'm the one who experiences it. I feel she's *trapped* in my house, and when she sees you there, she wants to reach out to you some way and the only way available is to slam doors. Maybe she wants you living in her house, rather than me. I believe she's reaching out to you for something. I just don't know what it is."

Garrett took her hand and felt strings tighten around his heart as he looked into her hypnotic blue eyes. He could get lost in those eyes forever.

"It's okay, sweetheart. Don't worry about Miss Rose. You can come to the ranch any time you want, and I assure you, she won't be there. There won't be any door slamming when you're at my house. Deal?"

He turned her hand over and kissed the underside of her wrist, and then placed his other hand over hers and covered it from view.

The warmth of his hands gave Emily an assurance she would always be safe with Garrett. In spite of all the misery she'd been through with Will, she now believed with her heart and soul that Garrett Loving was a man with strong character and integrity who could be trusted. She looked into the depths of his expressive eyes that shown as though lit from within. His full lips brushed hers ever so slightly and gave her butterflies.

"Now," he said," let's go take a look in my storage building and see what we can find for Miss Emily's house."

Chapter Sixteen

Garrett carried the conversation as they drove back to his ranch. Emily's mind attempted to wrap around the second time she heard him say he wanted her with him permanently. Did permanently mean marriage? With that elusive question in mind, she closed her eyes and drifted off to sleep with her head resting against his shoulder.

"Emily, we're here," Garrett said as he kissed her on the top of her head. "You dozed off on the way home. You're sure you want to do this now? I can rummage for the tools tomorrow if you're too tired tonight."

"I'm okay. Let's go take a look."

The storage building stood behind the barn and stables. Garrett pulled keys from his pocket and opened the lock with a click.

"Let me turn on the light. It's pretty crowded in here, and I don't want you to trip over anything."

A flip of the switch illuminated the entry room from two long bright fluorescent light fixtures on the ceiling. The storage building was large and included several rooms. Each room was full of boxes, tools, old toys and a couple of desks. Although there was a lot of stuff stashed away there, it was stacked and stored neatly. Most of the boxes were labeled.

"Here they are," Garrett said as he triumphantly held up a small shovel and rake.

"There are several other things here we could probably use. Want to browse a bit before we go? If there's anything in here you want, please feel free to take it. This stuff has been stored here for six years. After Mom died, I had the cleaning lady pack her personal effects and I brought them here for storage. I also brought the boxes from the attic, yet I've never gone through any of them. Maybe you can help me do that. How about it, Emily? Want to go on a treasure hunt? Or, maybe we should call it a scavenger hunt, since I'm not sure what we'll find."

Emily and Garrett worked through the next hour, opening boxes, looking through clothing, shoes, knickknacks, and assorted memorabilia. Garrett had started a box with *Keep* scrawled in black marker, one with the word *Donate* and another labeled *Emily,* since she expressed a wish to keep some of the things that belonged to Miss Rose. She filled her box with vintage handbags, shoes, delicate handmade handkerchiefs, a couple of crocheted shawls and a box of old postcards and notes.

"Are you sure you don't want to keep any of her things from my box?" she asked Garrett.

He picked up the box and carried it to his truck. "I kept what I wanted. Feel free to do as you please with the things in your box and get anything else you want.

"It's getting late, Emily. Do you want me to drive you home? I can unload this box at your house. Then I'll pick you up tomorrow and bring you back to get your car. I would love to cook dinner for you tomorrow evening. Will that be okay with you?"

Emily had forgotten her car was parked in front of Garrett's house. She didn't like to drive at night, and she did want to see him again the next day. In fact, she wanted to see him on a regular basis. She was glad she'd made the phone call to repair the damage done by her hasty escape. She was also glad he understood about Will and the feeling of betrayal that left her feeling so conflicted about romance.

"I'd love for you to cook dinner for me tomorrow night, and I'll cook dinner for you the next night. Does that plan meet with your approval?"

She felt his arms close around her again, the masculine fragrance he wore tantalizing, the pressure of his lips against hers when they kissed.

It was all Emily could do to pull away from the heat of Garrett's arms. "We should probably go before we forget what we're doing here."

He drove her home and carried her box of retro treasures inside the house, asking, "What time should I pick you up tomorrow?"

"Late afternoon. About four-thirty?"

She would fill her time going through the box of Miss Rose's things. It might keep her mind off Garrett during the day. In addition, she had errands to run and chores to do, so she could stay occupied until he came to pick her up.

Garrett gathered her to him at the front door for a goodnight kiss.

"I'll be lonely until we're together again, darlin'. I love looking into your beautiful eyes. I love the way you brush your hair from your face. I love the way you get that little wrinkle in your forehead when you're deep in thought, but most of all, I love having you in my arms. I love you, Emily Parker, and I don't want to let you go."

He pulled her closer and brushed her hair with his lips. She felt the feathery light touch on her hair, and then he laced his hands through it and cupped her head as he brought his lips to hers again before releasing her.

"I'll see you tomorrow at 4:30 on the dot. Until then, think about me . . . about us."

And he was gone.

Emily dressed for bed, all the while thinking about her evening with Garrett. He made it very clear that he cared for her, that he loved her and wanted her to be a permanent part of his life. She'd asked him to go slowly, so she must wait until he explained what he meant by that word *permanent.* It was obvious they both wanted to work out their relationship. She knew now it was important to both of them. Yes, she could be patient. Good things are worth the wait.

Tired and happy, she drifted off to sleep but was awakened by a slamming door. *Bam!* Sitting up in bed, she switched on the lamp and let her eyes adjust to the light. She saw nothing outside her bedroom door, so she padded barefoot into the living room. She felt a chill as she walked to the fireplace. She knew the temperature was pleasant outside, and she hadn't needed a coverlet in her bedroom. The weather was at that stage where there was no need for either air conditioning or heat. Yet, cold air crawled up her body from the floor and touched each vertebra in her back as it made its way to her neck and up her jaws. Looking around, she saw nothing out of place, but the chill left as she stood near the box she'd brought home from Garrett's.

"What is it, Miss Rose?" she asked aloud. "Are you angry that your son and I made up and want to be together? Don't you want him to be happy, or is it that I'm not socially acceptable to you? Give me a sign or something that I can hold onto. I love your son, and he loves me. So there! Just go away and leave us alone."

I'm talking to a ghost? Do I expect her to answer? How will I know if she does?

She sank into the nearest overstuffed chair and dropped her head into her hands. The enormity of this haunting situation was getting on her nerves.

What does she want? Why is she continuing to annoy me with the slamming doors? I can't read her mind!

Emily had no clue what her ghost was thinking or why she was still here. She'd read stories about spirits remaining in a house because of unfinished business. Was that why Miss Rose was still in her house? Did she have unfinished business?

Is your unfinished business with Garrett, or is it with me?

She thought about her doors slamming each time she'd been with Garrett, or after he was in her house, the doors not opening when she tried them, but Garrett having no problem with them.

She must be concentrating on me, but why? What does she want? Is she trying to tell me something? What in the world could it be? Do I need a Ouija board or a medium? Me? The skeptic who never believed in any of that paranormal stuff?

Emily raised her head and her eyes stopped at the box she'd brought home.

"Maybe there's a clue in here," she said aloud, as if there was someone else in the room and she wasn't there alone with a ghost.

A beautiful orchid shawl was the first thing she pulled out. Unfolding it and wrapping it around her cool shoulders, she thought it looked like a prayer shawl. She knew Miss Rose was active in church, and Garrett told her his mother did a lot of charity work for the community.

Emily pulled the lightweight shawl closer around her shoulders to banish the chill still in the room. She lifted a pair of soft leather shoes from the box and placed them on her feet. She was surprised that they fit perfectly and warmed her bare feet.

Next was a box of note cards. Opening them, she found written notes from a variety of people. She was surprised Garrett would hand his mother's personal messages over to her without first reading them. Perhaps he wasn't aware what they were and she should show them to him.

Emily switched on the side table lamp as she picked up one of the notes and read it. It was a thank-you note from someone Miss Rose helped with a fundraiser. Another one was a birthday

card from her church, and several were
get-well cards.

One card had a handwritten message: "Thank you so much for your contribution to our fundraiser. These funds will help offset our hospital bill for little Aaron."

Another person—a woman—said she loved the cake Miss Rose baked for her when she was feeling down. And several people thanked her for allowing them to have a birthday party in her yard. It seemed Miss Rose helped a lot of people, and many acknowledged her good deeds with cards.

Emily's eye lids began to feel heavy, so she carefully laid everything back in the box and placed it, along with the shawl, inside the larger box and closed the lid. She couldn't think about this anymore tonight. She would deal with it the next day.

I feel like Scarlett O'Hara. Tomorrow I'll think of some way . . . after all, tomorrow is another day.

Chapter Seventeen

Emily awoke with thoughts of Miss Rose and her charitable ways. Maybe she'd misjudged the woman, considering her simply an obsessive mother. Now she didn't know what to think. Most people were not all good or all bad, but a mixture of many traits that made up their personality and character. Miss Rose obviously had many good ways, in spite of her obsession with running Garrett's life.

Emily's day was busy with tasks around the house. There were always many things to do indoors when seasons changed, and she busied herself doing them. She put light slipcovers on the living room furniture, replaced some heavy drapes with lightweight ones over sheer panels. Busy work, but it all needed to be done. She felt quite virtuous when she ticked all these things off her To-Do list.

She couldn't run errands with her car at the ranch, so time began to drag. Emily's mind wandered back and forth from her tasks to the box that contained items belonging to Miss Rose. Would anything else there hold the answer to her questions?

Finally, she succumbed to her curiosity and, placing a fresh cup of coffee on a side table, she set the box in front of her and began to sort through it. She had already pulled out the shawls and the box of notes. There wasn't anything in them to signify the former owner's feelings one way or the other. The shoes fit Emily perfectly, which seemed strange—that her feet slid so smoothly into Miss Rose's shoes—and she loved the shawls.

She pulled out a couple of vintage handbags and placed them in her lap. One was a white baroque with beads that formed a rose on one side of the purse, and the other was brown velveteen with a gold clasp and pleats on one side.

Emily held the white purse up to see the intricate work of the beading. She could tell this had been one of Miss Rose's favorites from the wear on the back and bottom of the bag. Tiny red beads were sewed in circles, and green ones made a triangle. Yellow and brown beads were in the center of the red circles. As she held it away from her, she could see the pattern. A red rose.

How appropriate. The rose must have been her signature design.

Emily liked the Victorian look of the handbag and decided she would hang it just below her glass-and-brass shelf in the bedroom. She laid it on the side table and reached for the brown purse.

She gently brushed her fingers down the pleats formed by the gathering of the material with the latch. The velveteen was smooth and didn't look worn at all. This bag apparently wasn't a favorite of the matriarch, yet when she opened it, Emily felt the same out-of-place coolness she had the previous last night.

The purse was dark and cold inside as she slowly slid her hand down into the silk lining. Almost afraid of what she would find, she quickly pulled her hand out and snapped it shut. She held it up and turned it around to inspect the back. It was flat on the back and she ran her fingers over the brass trim that covered the top opening. Her heart beat nervously like a bongo drum. Why did she feel so much anxiety when she opened the bag?

Emily carefully placed the brown velveteen bag on her lap and stared at it while her mind recollected the strange events she'd experienced since moving into Miss Rose's house. The first time she heard the door slam was when the real estate agent was showing her the property. She hadn't been able to open the door for several minutes. Later, when Garrett tilled her garden spot and stayed for supper, she had been awakened by a door slamming, and it happened again each time after that whenever he spent time with Emily.

She slowly stroked the soft fabric of the bag and tried to put a prospective on the actions of . . . what? Who? The resident ghost?

I know this was your home, Miss Rose, but you're dead and don't need it. Dead people don't belong in earthly houses. Why aren't you in Heaven where you should be? Besides, the house is mine now. My name is on the deed.

How could she, Emily Parker, a normally sensible woman, allow herself to believe the ghost of Miss Rose existed in this or any other house?   Why was she carrying on a one-sided conversation with a wraith, a spirit, an invisible presence? Was she setting herself up for a nervous breakdown?

Lifting the handbag's catch, she resolutely peered inside, pulled out a handkerchief and carefully unfolded it, admiring the handiwork. The embroidery was intricate, and there were pink roses in one corner. She lifted it to her cheek and felt the softness and smelled the sweet aroma of scented tea roses.   The handkerchief must have lain in a drawer with a sachet full of rose petals.

Beautiful, she thought as she carefully laid it aside and again slid her hand inside the dark valley to feel for anything else left in the bag. Her hand touched paper. She was excited as she carefully pulled the yellowed envelope from the bag and examined it. It was not addressed to anyone. There was no writing on it at all. Did she dare open it? Was it a private note meant for someone else's eyes? Was she intruding?

Alas, curiosity got the better of her, and Emily very carefully opened the envelope—not difficult because the glue had dried—and pulled out two pages of a handwritten letter. The stationary was from a small tablet like the one she remembered her grandmother using. It was no bigger than a five-by-seven sheet with blue lines, and the top still had residual red glue where it had been torn from a tablet.

Emily carefully folded the bottom down and held it with her thumb and forefinger. With her other hand, she raised the top and began to read the spidery handwriting that wavered as though the hand writing it shook:

My darling son,

I write this letter to you knowing I am not long for this world. My hope is that you will find it at the appropriate time you need to hear what I must say to you.

You have been the light in my life since the day you were born. I felt like I had been given a wonderful gift when you arrived all pink and smiling. I never wanted you out of my sight, and I always had you by my side. I never allowed anyone to babysit with you. Instead, I invited your friends to visit our home so that you were always with me.

My son, I know I was too possessive of you and kept you too close to home, but I had such a fear that I would lose you if you were out of my sight that I pulled you closer and closer as you grew older.

You were a wonderful little boy, inquisitive, happy, loving the outdoors, but most of all, compassionate. You brought many a stray animal home and convinced me that it would die if we didn't let the poor creature stay, and we always did.

Oh, you had your days as you grew from an adolescent to a young man, but I knew they were just growing pains. I watched you grow into a wonderful young man and knew that one day you would meet someone who would take my place in your life. I couldn't allow that to happen. There was not one woman who could love you as much as your own loving mother.

I'm sorry for many of the girls that I turned away from you. I now realize I was wrong in my thinking, but I felt I had to protect you from their feminine wiles, for you see, dear, they only wanted to take you away from me, and I couldn't allow that.

My wish, now that I have but a short time left, is that you will find someone who will love you as you deserve. Even though I will soon be gone from your sight, I will not give up my quest to guide you to the woman who is right for you. I will gather my determination and strength of will before my life force ebbs away so that I can fulfill this final loving duty for my cherished son.

Even though I will be gone, and you will know I'm gone, I will somehow, in some way, get the message to you when you find the woman who is truly right for you. I'm not sure how I will do that, but rest assured I will find a way to get your attention, my dear son.

Take care, my darling boy, and know that Mommy loves you and will always look out for your best interests. Don't forget, I will watch over you and let you know when you've found the one woman who can love you as you deserve, who will be caring and true to you for the rest of your life.

My love forever,

Mother (Miss Rose)

Emily read the letter over again and then sat clutching it to her chest. She felt tears sting her eyes just before they spilled over and ran down her cheeks.

How this woman must have loved her son and how fearful she was of losing him. So fearful that she couldn't leave this earth until he was with the person she felt would make him happy and keep him safe just as she had done for all those years. Does she consider me that person?

Emily knew every mother's fear was that her children might be unhappy, and she worried about their safety. She felt sadness in her heart for Garrett's mother, who had lost her husband and then found it so difficult to let go of her only son.

"Oh, Miss Rose," she said aloud, "I'll take care of your son. I'll love him and keep him happy and safe for as long as I live. I won't let you down. That's a promise."

Still clutching the letter, she embraced the peace and quiet of the room and suddenly realized the temperature was warm. Did the door slams mean Miss Rose approved of her, or was it the opposite? Did she want Emily in Garrett's life or out of his life? How would she know? Did she have to prove herself to Miss Rose in some way before she would be satisfied and leave them to their happiness?

Emily was startled out of her daze by the doorbell. She wiped the wetness from her eyes and headed for the front door. When she opened it, Garrett was standing on the porch. He put his hands gently on her shoulders.

"What's wrong, Emily? Why are you crying? Did Forrester contact you?"

"Will . . .?" she repeated, still not in the moment. "Oh. Will. No, there's nothing from Will, but you aren't going to believe what I found in your mother's purse."

She walked back to the sofa and collapsed into its cushions. Garrett sat beside her, and she handed him the yellow paper she had been clutching to her chest. She watched as he read the letter from his beloved mother. She saw his face go white and then cloud over. She desperately wanted to know what he was thinking, but didn't want to interrupt this moment between mother and son, the words written when the mother was facing death as a message to her dearly loved son, now a message to him from beyond the grave. He sat on the sofa beside Emily, not moving, with a glazed look on his face as if he had gone back in time. She couldn't fathom his mood, but she waited for him to speak.

"Emily, I don't know what to say. I haven't truly believed you about doors slamming and my mother's ghost being in this house. I'm sorry for that. I'm not sure what to think of this letter. I need to process it for a while, but in the meantime, I'd like you to come home with me, just in case she is still in this house. Will you do that?"

"Yes," she said, as he stood and pulled her from the sofa into his arms.

"I loved my mother, but if you need protection from her spirit, I'll protect you. Until I can figure out whether she is in favor of you or against you, I don't want you staying here. Pack your overnight bag with enough to last a few days, and let's leave right now. I don't want you to spend another night here alone."

Emily went into her bedroom as Garrett checked the other doors to be sure they were locked. She packed her overnight bag and started out the bedroom door just as she saw it begin to close. Grabbing at the door knob to keep it open, she caught her foot on a rug beside the bed. The door slammed. As hard as she tried, she couldn't open it.

That's it, then . . . Miss Rose is telling me she doesn't want me with her son. I don't meet her standards.

Hoping Garrett hadn't gone outside, she yelled for him. He came bounding through the door and looked around the room. His look of concern calmed her nerves.

"Are you okay? I heard you call out."

"I'm fine, now. I turned to go out the door, it slammed in my face, and I couldn't open it. It frightened me. I'm glad it opened for you."

He reached for her bag. "Come on. Let's go, Emily. Right now."

He guided her from the bedroom through the house to the front door and out onto the porch, firmly closing the door behind them and turning the key in the lock.

Garrett turned out of the driveway and headed his truck toward the ranch. Emily looked back at the house, watching it grow smaller in the distance and fade into the night like a forgotten dream. She felt safe, confident in Garrett's promise that he would protect her from his mother, whether she was indeed a restless spirit or her strong personality merely lived on in her son's memory. Miss Rose was in the past where she belonged, and Emily was headed toward her future with Garrett. She thought about that future and smiled.

As the truck disappeared into the still Texas night and stars twinkled far above the windshield, there was a slight movement of the front bedroom curtain back in Miss Rose's house.

But there was no one around to see it. Emily and Garrett were gone.

--THE END--

Excerpt from

"Miss Rose's Boy"

The Spirit of Miss Rose, Book Two

One foot in front of the other, Emily told herself as she walked the grassy pathway leading to the man who was about to become her husband. She could see Garrett Loving waiting for her at the end of the outdoor aisle. The smile on his face and the twinkle in his blue eyes made her heart leap with joy. It was obvious he felt the same as she did today.

"I now pronounce you husband and wife." The preacher said, paused and then smiled.

"You may kiss your bride."

There were titters from the guests as the kiss lengthened and Garrett hugged Emily closely to his chest.

"Ladies and gentlemen, may I introduce Mr. and Mrs. Garrett Loving."

Garrett held Emily's hand as they walked toward the ranch house for the reception, their guests laughing and talking all around them. Their decision to have the ceremony on the grassy knoll behind the house had been ideal. It was the perfect spot to say their vows with the view of a beautiful bluff complete with hundreds of trees that would soon become a virtual painting of gold shades, greens and browns. On this beautiful autumn day with a few early-falling leaves swirling around her feet, Emily Parker became Mrs. Garrett Loving.

* * *

A month later, Garrett unlocked the door, swept Emily into his arms and carried her across the threshold. Like the true southern gentleman he was, her new husband gently sat her on the sofa, removed his hat and, with a sweeping bow, said, "Welcome home, Mrs. Loving."

"Thank you Mr. Loving. I can't believe we've been gone four weeks. You have to admit, a month in Italy is a long honeymoon, but I enjoyed every minute of it and will treasure our time together there."

"Nothing but the best for my bride. I've waited a long time to find the person I want to spend the rest of my life with, and you, Mrs. Loving, are the right person. I wanted our beginning to be a memorable one, and I plan for us to have many more adventures together in the coming years."

* * *

"We've been back from our honeymoon a week today, Emily." Garrett said, peering over his paper at his wife. "Are you still happy to be with me here at the ranch?"

"Of course I am, darling. I love living at the ranch and watching all the activity that goes on here each day. Now I understand the meaning of a working ranch. How much longer can you telecommute before you're needed at your office in Dallas?"

"I need to go in tomorrow. You can go with me or stay here and get settled in here . . . browse around, change anything you like to suit your tastes."

Emily thought for a moment before she spoke, "I think I'll stay here if you don't mind. I need to drive into Cedar Valley and check on my house."

"Have you decided what you're going to do with it?"

"No. I'm not sure if I want to keep it or sell it, since it doesn't matter to you, but I don't have to make up my mind just yet."

The next day, Emily pulled into the driveway of her little cottage. She still loved to see the large oak trees in the front of the house. The leaves were a riot of autumnal color.

Unlocking the back door, Emily stepped into the den and immediately felt a chill. The weather was beginning to turn cold, but she knew the central heat was on with the thermostat on a comfortable setting, so the house should be warm.

It wasn't as if she hadn't previously felt that mysteriously cold atmosphere inside this house. Walking through the rooms to her bedroom, she felt the chill race up her spine and dance on her cheeks. Wrapping her arms around her shivering shoulders, she walked into the room she'd claimed as hers when she first moved into the cottage. The door slammed behind her so suddenly she barely got out of its way.

"So, you're still here, Miss Rose. I thought, or maybe I just hoped, you'd be gone by now."

Emily's voice echoed in the closed room. She reached for the knob to open the door, but to no avail. Sitting on her bed resignedly, she looked around the room to see if anything was out of place—anything that foretold the presence of a ghost.

"Miss Rose, I'm your son's wife now, so you can rest in peace, and just to let you know, I'm thinking of selling your . . . er . . . my house. Will you remain here if a new family moves in, or will you go away as you should have done many years ago? Garrett and I won't be living here, so there's no need for you to linger."

Emily heard her cellphone ring and grabbed the door knob again. She marveled at how easily it opened, and then hurried into the hallway where she'd left the phone on a table.

"Hello?"

"Hi, Emily—Stan here. When did you get back from your

honeymoon?"

She was surprised to hear her brother's voice. He and his wife JacQue had moved to Boston three years earlier for his job. She hadn't seen them in nearly a year, nor had she talked to them since before the wedding, which they were unable to attend.

"We've been back for a week. I'm at my house trying to decide what to do with it."

"Are you going to sell it or keep it?"

"I'm not sure. I love the house, but also don't want it to leave it empty."

"How about renting it to us? You can always sell it later if that's what you decide to do."

"You and JacQue? You're moving back to Texas?"

"My company is opening a new branch in Wichita Falls. We need a place to stay for maybe six months or so, and your house is the first one I thought of since it's vacant. What do you think? Will you rent it to us for the short term?"

"Of course I will. That way, I won't have to decide what to do with it for a while. When do you plan to move?"

"As soon as possible, Em. I'll let you know in a day or two the exact date to expect us."

He described his plans for the new venture and said how glad he and his wife would be to get back to their home state.

When the call ended, Emily thought about having Stan and JacQue live in the cottage and felt it was the answer to her dilemma—at least temporarily.

She pressed the speed-dial number for Garrett and was pleased when he answered immediately. She told him about her brother's call and how glad she was that she need not make a decision about the house for a while. He said to expect him at the ranch about eight that evening and she could tell him all about her day.

126

Later, as he walked through the ranch house door, Garrett put his arms around Emily and said, "I missed you today, my love. Now, tell me about your day in addition to Stan's phone call. Did you have time to visit your house?"

Should she tell him about Miss Rose slamming the door behind her at the cottage, or not? They had promised each other there would be no secrets between them. There was her answer. No secrets meant complete disclosure.

"Yes, I went to the cottage, and when I walked into the back door, Garrett, I felt a chill right away. Then I went into the bedroom, and the door slammed behind me. I tried to open it and couldn't. But when my cell phone rang in the other room, I had no problem opening the door."

Garrett looked at her with a question in his eyes. "Did you check the thermostat to make certain the heat was still on and there were no windows open?"

"I checked the heat first thing, and there weren't any windows open. Chills crept up my spine when I went into the bedroom, and the door slamming was just like before. I'm sure it was Miss Rose there to haunt me."

Emily's jaw was firm as she finished her account. "She's still there, Garrett, waiting for me."

"What about your brother? Will you tell him about Miss Rose?"

"No, I don't think so. I'm anxious to see if she reveals herself to anyone other than me."

She chuckled. "Stan is easily spooked, so I didn't want to alarm him. He said they want to move as soon as possible, so I'll thoroughly clean the house, let Miranda choose any of my furniture she wants and store the remainder to get the place ready for them."

*   *   *

Emily's brother, Stan, and his wife flew into Dallas the following Friday and were met at the Dallas-Ft. Worth airport by Garrett. He drove them to Cedar Valley to see the house, already emptied and sparkling clean, where JacQue sketched the layout and took measurements for furniture placement. Charmed by the cottage, lawns and rose bushes, she was vocal in her enthusiasm and looking forward to living there.

Afterward, they went out to the ranch to visit for the rest of weekend. Garrett showed Stan around the property and stables while the two women pored over photographs of the wedding and videos taken in Italy.

The weekend was pleasant, with Miranda, Jared and a growing Chris—now crawling—joining them on Saturday for a barbeque with all the trimmings. Garrett, who grew up as an only child, warmed to the idea of his new extended family by marriage.

Two weeks later Stan and JacQue arrived in Cedar Valley with the moving van pulling in just behind them at the house. They were slightly behind schedule because of a flat tire in a small Tennessee town that meant waiting until an auto store opened the next morning. Otherwise, their trip from the northeast was uneventful. They were eager to get settled before Stan left for Wichita Falls to oversee startup operations of the new company branch. JacQue had a diagram all ready for the movers, who had their belongings inside and arranged in record time.

Stan and JacQue were now the new residents of Miss Rose's house.

Watch for **Miss Rose's Boy**
The Spirit of Miss Rose
Book Two

Coming soon

.